The Last Outbreak

AWAKENING

JEFF OLAH

Cover design by Rebecca Frank
(http://rebeccafrank.design)

. . .

Visit the author's website for free stories, behind the
scenes extras and much more.
www.JeffOlah.com

ISBN-13: 978-1533516138
ISBN-10: 1533516138

BOOKS BY JEFF OLAH

The Dead Years Series:
ORIGINS

THRESHOLD

TURBULENCE

BLACKMORE

COLLAPSE

VENGEANCE

HOMECOMING

RETRIBUTION

ABSOLUTION

The Last Outbreak Series:
AWAKENING

DEVASTATION

DESPERATION

REVOLUTION

SALVATION

More Stories:
RATH

INTENT

The End of the World was Only
the Beginning

The Last Outbreak...

Many have asked about the connection between this new series *The Last Outbreak* and the previous series *The Dead Years* and how the two are related. Below are a few questions that should clear things up. (There's also a sneak peek of *The Dead Years* at the conclusion of this book.)

Q: Can you give us a brief description of *The Last Outbreak*?

A: Sure, *The Last Outbreak* is a story of survival set in a small fictional town, a few hours outside a larger, more densely populated metropolitan city. The story will follow the lives of a small group of individuals as they progress through what's left of the world following the Zombie Apocalypse chronicled in the Best-Selling Post-Apocalyptic Thriller, *The Dead Years*.

Q: Speaking of *The Dead Years*, is it necessary that one reads this series first to enjoy *The Last Outbreak*?

A: I'm actually glad this question came up. It is not

necessary to read *The Dead Years* first. The two series are complete stories and as such, stand alone in their own right. They are built in the same world and will have definite tie-ins, although nothing will be lost if you read one particular series before or after the other.

Q: Okay... *The Dead Years*, what is that?
A: *The Dead Years* is the Best-Selling Post-Apocalyptic Zombie series written between March of 2013 and June of 2015. There are eight books in total, which follow a small group of survivors as they traverse the worst plague the earth has ever seen. These individuals quickly realize that the flesh-devouring zombies are not the only thing to fear in this new world.

Q: Regarding *The Last Outbreak*; is the entire series set in just one location?
A: Another great question. I can see how one might gather that from the brief description above, however, without giving away too much, I can definitively say that not only will the characters break out of their small town, but they will also travel far and wide in search of what they believe to be the answers they are seeking. (It's gonna get rough for these people pretty quickly.)

Q: How long will this new series be?
A: The series is scheduled for a five book run. It may go shorter and it may just go longer. It all depends on

what the characters decide to do in their journey to Salvation. I'm going to throw this new group into impossible situations, watch what they do, and then report back. All I can say for certain is that it will not be an easy road for these survivors.

Q: Where can we find the rest of these books?
A: As each new book is released, it will be uploaded to my author page on Amazon. Although, if you'd like to get an instant notification when each new book hits the shelves at Amazon, you can join my Exclusive Reader Group and be among the first to pick up the new series. (Sign up at JeffOlah.com)

*I hope this intro to the new series is helpful, and as always, I thank you for your support and can't wait to hear what you all think of *The Last Outbreak.*

- Jeff Olah

PROLOGUE

Exactly ten minutes early, Emma Runner strode into the twenty-thousand square foot privately owned hanger of BXF Technologies. Sitting in silence, a pair of Gulfstream G280s waited to usher her away from the city. Moving quickly across the red and white polished concrete floor, she avoided eye contact with the pilot, now staring down at her from the cabin door. She instead moved toward the black, Italian leather sofa situated along the rear wall, dropped her bags, and reached for her phone.

Entering her pass code, she glanced back at the pilot and held up an index finger. He nodded and disappeared back into the jet. Returning to the backlit screen, she stared at the message icon and shook her head. And because her OCD would eat her alive if she dropped her phone back into her bag, she opened the app to confirm there were no new messages. "Come on Ethan."

Before closing out her messages, she re-read the most recent and swallowed hard. Why would we need to leave tonight? Why at four in the morning, and why back to the West Coast? They'd only arrived a week earlier, and she'd just gotten used to the new time zone. However, these were questions she'd have to keep to herself. After hearing the story about the last person to interrogate the man running this company, she didn't need another reason to continue down that path.

Running on less than two hours of sleep, she was exhausted. Even the four cups of superheated caffeine were making little headway in reviving her from last night's client dinner. She was initially nervous to meet the businessmen from the other side of the continent, and for the first few hours, she only spoke when absolutely necessary.

.   .   .

The men were introduced as Maxwell Amador and Gerald Fienberg. All she was told was that they helped fund the new project she'd be assigned to, and that they were given only base-level information, and promised a five-hundred percent return once the end product hit the battlefield.

As the lead chemist, the investors from the East Coast demanded that she attend. And although she hadn't completely familiarized herself with the project, the science behind the injectable was something that she believed to be at least ten years off. The men who were to invest nearly a billion dollars would be looking for specifics, although she was instructed to keep it simple—and under no circumstances was she to reveal what the true capabilities of the program were.

Coming in near the unofficial launch of Project

Ares, she understood that she'd been the fourth to take on the position. However, the fate of the first three chemists, along with any indication as to who they were, was kept private. She didn't care. This was her break, and she didn't see fit to question the company willing to pay her twice what she was asking.

An hour prior to last night's dinner meeting, seated in the backseat of the jet-black Rolls-Royce Phantom, she sank into the buttery, crème-colored leather. And as the man who signed her checks scrolled quickly through his phone, she awaited his instruction.

Standing nearly six feet tall, his thick salt and pepper hair, chiseled features, and lean frame lent credence to the H. Huntsman suit he'd decided on for the evening. The man seated to her left finished with the details of his message, checked the time, and then turned to her with a grin that only slightly put her at ease. "Emma Runner... do you think you're ready for this?"

"Mr. Goodwin, I would first like to express to you my gratitude for the opportunity to—"

His slight smile began to morph into something resembling confusion. And Emma's short sermon fell off abruptly as he shook his head. "Listen, I'm a man who has little time for anything other than forward movement. You've already proven worthy of this job, and this trip. There was no need to thank me or anyone else when you were initially hired and there isn't one now."

"Yes sir."

"My name is Marcus Goodwin. Formalities can wait until we are back in that other time zone. For now, let's focus on making sure the men who are handing over the check are satisfied with the explanation we have to offer."

"Sure, but how exactly are we going to explain what this program is all about—I mean the physical details can be a bit complicated?"

"We aren't."

"No?"

"Not tonight," Goodwin said. "Tonight we make sure they're comfortable accepting that what we are doing is going to change the world. Make them believe it, make them beg me to let them invest."

Smiling apprehensively as the car slowed, Emma turned and peered out her window, still unclear about exactly what he wanted and why she was flown across the country. "It looks like we're here."

Before responding, he leaned in, laid his hand on her left knee, and let it drift up her thigh. "Once this investor is secured, we'll be completely self-regulating. No agencies to dictate the how's and why's. Those other contracts will be burned. And if another politician ever steps foot in our building, it'll be for an interview. Tonight I need you to—"

His phone's ringing sliced through the tension, and Emma drew her left leg back. Straightening in his seat, he looked at the screen and shook his head. "Daniels," he said under his breath. "What the hell does he want?"

As the car rolled to a stop, he stayed seated, as Emma's door was opened from the outside and she exited. Placing the phone to his ear, his door was also opened. "Daniels," he said, "what are you still doing—"

"Yes, I'm meeting with them tonight."

Looking down at his watch and then back through the open door, he stepped out and started for the entrance. He marched across the busy sidewalk and paused before the entrance as Emma moved inside. "No, that couldn't be us. Trust me, there's nothing to worry about. I don't care what you're hearing. And yes, they've been trying to reach me all afternoon. However, I have a few things to take care of. I'll call them when I get back to the room tonight. You just head home and take care of—"

Holding the phone out away from his ear, he again checked his watch. "Yes, I'm well aware of your title. You've made sure of that over the last few years," his voice intensifying, "but you need to remember that I don't answer to you... any of you."

Looking over his shoulder, he could see through the crowded restaurant and into the bar. The deep pockets he was there to meet had already spotted Emma and were quickly approaching. "No, I haven't been watching the news, I've been out here on the other side of the country attempting to keep this thing afloat. When I get back in town at the end of next week, I'm coming up there to throw you and everyone else out of my facility."

Staring through the floor-to-ceiling, plate-glass

window as it gathered arcs of frost in each of its four corners, Goodwin could feel his heart beating in his ears. "Do what you have to, although you know who I am, and what I'm capable of. Just make sure that you and your people are gone by the time I arrive."

Ending the call, he slid his phone into his pocket, straightened his tie, and walked into the crowded bar.

.   .   .

Having scrolled through each message twice, she paused on the final text from her mother and read it once again. Sweetheart, your father is ill, and at the moment I just want him to rest. I'm shutting off the phones and will call you in the morning. Have a safe trip, we love you. Mom and Dad.

As the door to the hanger slammed shut, Emma dropped her phone into her bag and turned toward the exit. He came through with the same exaggerated stride as earlier, although he was different. Much different.

Moving quickly to the second jet at the far end of the open air hanger, Marcus Goodwin spoke quickly to the unidentified man at his side. As Emma tossed her bag over her shoulder and started at a right angle toward the jet, he didn't appear to notice her existence.

"Mr. Goodwin, are we—"

He didn't acknowledge her; instead, he turned to the much smaller man who trailed by at least two paces and pointed at his plane. "James, let the pilot know that we need to be in the air within five minutes. I don't want to hear any excuses. Once airborne, I need you to gain access to the offices and make sure we're ready. The next few days are going to be interesting."

As the smaller man moved away, Emma hurried to Goodwin's side. "Sir, what are we doing here? Do I need to begin—"

Stopping at the stairs to the second jet, Goodwin finally turned and acknowledged her. "I'm leaving."

"We're leaving... right?"

"Yes and no. I'm leaving in this plane and going back to the office. I've got a few things to take care of in the coming days, and will come for you when the time is right."

"Wait," Emma said. "What do you mean come for me? I thought I was leaving as well."

"You are; however, you're getting on that other jet and going home—to your house. I have arranged for a private security team to stay with you until I'm able to bring you to a safe place. I don't have time to go through everything right now, although I want you to—"

"Safe place?" Emma's mouth went dry and as her knees began to falter, she questioned the cause. Was it from the punishing exhaustion brought on by her lack of sleep, or this new look of desperation poisoning Goodwin's expression? She was willing to bet every penny she'd earned over the last year that it was the former. The man standing less than two feet away had little use for such emotion.

Pulling out his phone as it again interrupted their conversation, Goodwin peered into the display and continued. "You haven't seen the news tonight?"

"No, why?"

"I'll have someone brief you on your flight back to Los Angeles. Just get home and stay put; I'll be in contact." Goodwin turned and quickly made his way into the plane, the door closing behind him.

Walking back to the idling jet reserved only for her, Emma withdrew her phone, keyed in her four character pass code and began checking her social media feed. Now stopped at the foot of the steps, she leaned into the railing and tried to ignore the icy tendrils climbing up her spine. "What. The. Hell?"

1

Early winter, approaching sunset...

Standing with his back to the wall, Ethan Runner wasn't yet ready to end his best friend's life.

The weapon hung loosely in his left hand. It was heavier than he remembered and now felt a bit awkward. Turning to the others, he said, "I can't do this."

No one said a word. Avoiding his gaze, the others had already made up their minds. They were done negotiating.

Shaking his head, he slowly raised the nine millimeter and placed it against David's temple. He'd run out of excuses for not doing what these people had demanded and the decision was no longer his to make. The four remaining survivors backed tightly into the rear of the vault had to take priority, and his best friend—were he still able—would have agreed.

Scanning the room, every expectant eye now focused elsewhere—the group had spoken. They not only wanted him to end what was left of his friend's life, they were also asking that Ethan do it now, before it was too late. Some were scared and a few had just run out of patience. The group already made it extremely clear how they felt, and given the fact that this was for the most part his idea, he had a hard time disagreeing.

Back to his friend, he stepped to the left and again checked the restraint. A five-foot section of audio cable tied around David's wrists didn't offer much in the way of security. He knew that. If what was happening out in the streets were to take hold of his friend, there would be little he or anyone else could do to stop what was coming.

"Do it! You know what's happening to him—just do it. You're putting everyone at risk." The outspoken drifter was finally putting a voice to what the group wanted to say.

Ethan didn't respond.

"Give me the gun, I'll do it." Mr. Outspoken, again living up to his moniker, couldn't seem to keep his mouth shut. Placing him at just shy of forty years old, his overly muscled frame and a month's worth of facial hair fit his exaggerated personality perfectly. Since entering the vault behind the two bank employees and pulling the door shut, he had yet to let up.

Ethan turned to the casually dressed man as his friend began to pull away. "Last time, keep quiet! You're the reason we're stuck in here. I'm not going to ask you again."

"Oh yeah I forgot, you're the big shot with the uniform and the badge. So tell me, what's your plan—huh?"

Ethan began to answer, but was cut short as the man continued. "You do realize that I just followed you and the others in here. And with those—those things outside the door, you're all real lucky I even thought to shut it behind us. If I hadn't, you'd all be dead or worse," Mr. Outspoken said, pointing at David. "You'd be just like him."

Turning away, he again focused on his friend. Sliding the pistol to David's forehead, he dropped to one knee, grabbed the back of his head, and pulled him in tight. "You don't deserve this. It should've been me." Ethan leaned in and placed his mouth just outside his friend's bloodstained ear. "I will get to Carly. I will get her somewhere safe. I promise you that."

His friend's body began to go rigid. Ethan felt David beginning to struggle. Leaning away and starting to stand, what little remained of his friend was now gone. The wounds along his right triceps oozed a yellowish-orange fluid that leaked out into the pool of coagulated blood surrounding their feet.

Peering into David's eyes, they were nearly unrecognizable as human. His once sapphire-blue eyes had faded into something just shy of translucent and were now obscured by a milky white haze. What lay behind the thick film was no longer the man with whom Ethan had spent the better part of his life. The fragments of his friend that still remained were quickly losing the battle with what had taken hold.

Beginning to growl, the beast now inching toward Ethan wore his friend's face, but most certainly was not him. Tugging at his makeshift restraints, the thing that David had become fought to free itself as the group collectively took a step back. Twisting against the weakened audio cable, his left arm, the less injured of the two, gave way.

The ensuing sound of bone on bone reverberated through the cramped vault. However, the realization that his friend had just broken his own arm in an attempt to free himself hung in the air with a bit more weight. What appeared to put an exclamation on the moment was the fact that David hadn't even flinched. Not in the slightest. He didn't look at the injury and only stared across the room at the five unbelieving individuals.

Turning from the others as he again raised the weapon, Ethan heard their gasps only just before he realized his friend was loose. With his hands now free, David shot forward as if out of a cannon. He slammed face-first into Ethan's chest, sending both men to the blood-soaked concrete floor, and Ethan's nine millimeter sliding into the corner.

Shielding himself from David's snapping jaws, Ethan drew his legs back into his chest and kicked straight up. He drove what used to be his friend's body back into the row of safety deposit boxes and twisted right in hopes of retrieving the weapon he'd just dropped. No luck—the only thing in his inverted field of view were the men and women now scrambling to either side.

As Ethan slid up and onto his knees, scanning the vault for his weapon, David shot forward yet again. Reflexively turning away, Ethan held out his right hand in hopes of deflecting the initial blow. He expected to be hit dead on and assumed that shortly following the collision he'd be flat on his back yet again. He envisioned his own demise, his friend tearing him apart without even the most remote chance of defending himself. This is where his life would end.

Clenching his jaw, he twisted to the right as David lunged forward yet again. The two bodies slammed into one another like wet bags of sand, sending Ethan back and into the bottom row of safety deposit boxes, the top of his head making contact first. Blinking through the pain, he attempted to draw in a deep breath and failed. This was it.

As his friend climbed on top and inched his way toward Ethan's face, his vision began to fade. Next, the low buzz in his ears told him that unconsciousness was not far off and if he hoped to walk out of the bank alive, he had to take some sort of action, only his arms were pinned to the floor below.

With David clawing his way up onto his chest, Ethan was only able to get glimpses of the battle he was losing. In between the shouts and screams, his mind waded in the shadows until it finally gave up. The last image to flash through his narrowed field of vision was the nine millimeter he'd held to his friend's head only moments before, and the glint of the barrel.

2

Eleven hours earlier...

After what Ethan had subjected himself to the prior night, no amount of sleep would have been sufficient to completely erase the damage. With his head placed ever so gently atop the costly memory-foam pillow, he could feel every individual hair on his head begging for mercy. He now regretted not downing the two glasses of water he was offered in between drinks.

Sliding his hand along the right side of the bed, and finally locating his phone, Ethan winced as he cracked his eyelids. Pulling the phone to his face, it cried out for the fourth time. Rolling onto his side, he silenced the phone and shoved it under the pillow. His alarm was always an unwelcome stranger, although this morning it came much too soon.

Out from under the warmth provided by his patchwork comforter, Ethan slowly dropped his legs over the side of the bed and placed his fingers against his eyes. Attempting to rub away the pain, he instinctively pulled back. The jackhammer working the inside of his skull had now decided it was time to turn up the intensity.

"Okay, that's not gonna work."

Pushing to stand, Ethan closed his eyes and waited as the room slowed its spin to a level that allowed him to start making forward progress. Driving his middle fingers into his temples somewhat made the trek to the kitchen a bit more bearable; however, in crossing the room and slamming his big toe into the forward bedpost, he stumbled into the door frame.

Speaking only to the gods of karma, he said, "Seriously? If this is what you're giving me, I'm goin' back to bed."

Taking a breath and peering out into the living room, he knew something was off. Daylight savings time had ended over a month ago, but that wasn't it. The absence of light seemed odd as he'd awoken at the same time every weekday for the last six months. He wasn't dreaming, or so he thought, although in his current condition there were no absolutes.

Accustomed to his new morning ritual, Ethan started for the light switch, and before noticing the time on the backlit desk clock, his attention was pulled back into his bedroom. The woman's scream from outside his bedroom window now fought for attention as his phone begged to be heard. Did the scream truly exist or was the unsettling sound just a memory? Again, he was at the mercy of too many tequilas from the night before.

Glancing into the kitchen before turning and

walking back to his room, Ethan was satisfied that at least his humble apartment hadn't suffered the usual carnage. Following the kind of night he and his co-worker usually had, he wasn't ever sure exactly what, or for that matter who, he'd find.

The smile on his face for not having destroyed anything within reach was short lived as his phone fired off its second call for attention. Shuffling the last three feet to the bed and falling face-first toward the ringing, Ethan inadvertently pushed his phone off the left side of the bed, silencing his nemesis. "Thank you."

Rolling onto his back, he reached toward the headboard, pulled his pillow back under his head, and closed his eyes.

Another scream, this time followed by a cry for help.

Ethan leaned onto his right side and craned his neck, attempting to get a glimpse of the commotion without actually leaving his bed. No such luck. All he was able to see were the distant street lamps and the glow they filtered into the night air. The city below would have to remain a mystery, at least for now.

"*Do not get involved,*" he said to himself. "*Do. Not. Get involved Ethan, you'll get out of bed and go to that window and if you see something, it'll be too late. You'll be in it. So, just lay here and don't move. In your condition, even if you did try to help these people, you'd probably just screw things up. Just stay here.*"

Back to his pillow for another sixty seconds, he lay motionless with his eyes closed, praying that whatever turmoil had begun outside his usually tranquil apartment building had concluded. *"Probably the Burkharts having another one of their late night discussions. If I had a nickel for every time those two lost their minds this past year, I'd be rich—and finally able to get the hell out of this town."*

With little doubt that his defeated body could do with another few hours of sleep, and still unsure of the exact time, his head was spinning. Remembering his phone still lay on the floor, Ethan rolled over and picked it up. Hitting the home button, he stared into the lighted display and shook his head at the three missed calls from his sister. "Emma."

His attention moving to the top and then right corner of the screen, he made a note of the time and the fact that he was left with only a one percent charge. Quickly pulling up the clock app and confirming that his alarm was still set, Ethan said. "What in the hell is so important at four a.m.?"

Placing his phone on the nightstand and plugging it in, he raked his hand through his dense, black mop of hair and gave into his curiosity. Again sliding out of bed, he moved to the window and pulled back the partially opened shade.

The first silhouetted figure moved quickly toward the area between the two apartment buildings and out of sight as Ethan caught a glimpse of the second. It moved much slower and if his sleep-deprived vision could be trusted, owned a considerable limp. *"This is new."*

As the second individual also disappeared into the

blank space, Ethan turned from the window and drew the shades. Pulling off his tee-shirt, he tossed it to the ground, pulled back the comforter, and climbed back into bed. "*Don't those idiots realize some people have to work in the morning*?"

Lying flat on his back, eyes closed and counting backward from one hundred as he drew in each new breath, Ethan focused only on welcoming the warm embrace of sleep. The mild pounding at the back of his head had an altogether different plan, and a slight advantage for keeping his attention.

"*Seventy-five...*" Also attempting to keep his mind from running through the possible scenarios playing out between the two obvious drunks outside his window, he continued his countdown.

"*Forty-eight...*" He'd usually never make it to sixty and as cloudy as his brain was rolling into bed a few hours ago, it amazed him that he'd awoken at all.

Out in the alley, the woman's voice returned. Only this time there were no cries for help, no frantic screaming. The only thing that remained were the bitter sobs usually indicating the conclusion of a night she'd surely regret.

As Ethan began to drift off, he doubted the next morning would be any kinder to him than it would be to the woman less than a hundred yards from his bedroom window.

3

The ground was still wet with what remained from the previous evening's snow when she and the others made their way through the gates and down to the loading area. It was cooler than she anticipated and although they were each allowed to wear a coat, the one she brought was dreadfully insufficient.

Tilting her head skyward and pushing her breath out into the morning air, she smiled as it momentarily crystallized and then drifted off into nothing. Being out of the building, while only for a few hours, changed her perspective. Having given up more times than she cared to count, today she wanted to be happy, to be like everyone else. Even if she wasn't. Something was happening and although no one was talking, she knew it was bad.

As the forty-five-foot bus rolled to a stop, Cora Adams looked up and down the line. The count hadn't changed since she'd checked it six times before. Having only heard rumors about where they were headed, the change in location was less exciting than it was unnerving. After what she'd seen before walking out into the cold morning air, she was almost looking forward to the trip.

Twenty-five passengers on a bus that was built to hold over four times that amount seemed like a waste. She wasn't about to question the directive handed down, although she had no idea why she was here or exactly what had taken place behind those gates she'd just walked through.

And as the line began to move forward, the images from the last few hours again played in her mind.

.   .   .

There were no specific instructions as they called out for her this morning. None that gave Cora any clue as to what was happening anyway. No one spoke, at least not to her or any of her friends. They only came, told them they were being transferred, and then gave them less than five minutes to get ready. Enough time to get ready, not enough to actually be ready.

Ms. Former Bodybuilder appeared out of the darkened hall. She asked that Cora and the others grab what they wanted. They were told to move as quickly as possible and be ready to board the bus in twenty minutes. No showers, no brushing your teeth, and if the bathroom was an absolute requirement, they'd better go now.

They were told to head toward the eastern end of the facility and not to stop for any reason. If the person in front of you or the person behind you

THE LAST OUTBREAK - AWAKENING

moved out of line, you were simply supposed to keep moving forward. "We wait for no one." According to Former Bodybuilder, their mass exit wouldn't be pretty, but it sure as hell was going to get the job done.

Tossing the only three items she still cared about into the plastic bag, Cora moved out into the hall and called for Trish. "Hey, let's go, I'm not sure what this is, but I don't think we want to stay around to find out."

The only friend she'd made since arriving here less than three months before sat frozen on her bed. She didn't respond. She didn't look up. She didn't move. She only clutched her left arm to her chest and cried. Trish never cried.

. . .

They met in the kitchen on Cora's second day. They worked side by side for three hours before Trish tossed a plate to the tiled floor and smiled. "Oops."

Cora raised an eyebrow and grinned.

"There are a set number of mistakes allowed from this kitchen before we have to answer for them. I haven't made one since last Monday and you seem to have your area under control, so I think we were due."

Back to the sink in front of her, Cora pulled out a short stack of three identical serving plates, raised them overhead, and slammed them to the ground. She turned back to her new friend and said, "I guess we may have something to answer for."

"I'm Trish, and I have a feeling we're gonna get along just fine."

Cora leaned back, brushed a long strand of hair away from her face, and checked both doors. "I'm just wondering what they'll do if we go beyond that number? What if we break ten plates, what about twenty? Who's gonna come 'talk' to us if we break every damn thing in this kitchen?"

"Well," her new friend said, "looks like someone's trying to get rid of their rookie card."

"Rookie card?"

"Yeah, happens to everyone when they first get here. Trying to prove you're something more than you were out there. Attempting to keep the others away. Hoping they'll see you as the little girl who isn't really a threat, or on the opposite end, someone who shouldn't be screwed with. Either way, they leave you alone."

Shaking her head, Cora said, "Just when I was starting to like you."

"Only trying to help." The woman roughly ten years her senior continued to smile. "I figure you're what, about five-foot-two and no more than a hundred pounds soaking wet? You've gotta admit the tough girl role is a bit of a stretch. Maybe you should just go with the innocent little girl thing. It's a bit more believable."

Cora began to respond, but was cut short as Trish added her final thought. "I like you, but you need to know where the line is."

"I'm sure I'll figure it out."

Back to the work staring her in the face, Trish nodded. "Yep, that's for sure, but just in case, I want you to know you can come to me if you need help."

·　·　·

The last few hours went by in the blink of an eye. The voices. The groans. The growls. The pleading. The crying. The distant sound of gunfire and finally the silence. Since arriving, she hadn't strung together more than three hours of sleep at any one time, although last night's foray into insomnia was much different.

Forced out into the hall and hurried along the dimly lit corridor, Cora was only able to catch quick glimpses of the sixteen silhouetted bodies lining the east wall. Laid head to toe and then again head to toe, they covered the length of the entire block wall. She turned away, moved closer to the women three feet ahead and didn't ask, mainly because she couldn't think of a single appropriate question.

Continuing through the set of double doors near the Control Center, Cora was overwhelmed by the distinct aroma of antiseptic spray and gauze bandages. Just on the other side of the inch-thick shatterproof glass stood four large men dressed in brightly colored hazmat suits and blacked-out masks. They paused as Cora and her group entered, but only for a brief moment.

The yellow suited men held back a separate line of women. One by one they placed a digital thermometer to the foreheads of the women. They paused, holding the readout to their masks, and either let them through to meet up with the others or pointed them back to the room they had just left. Each was given a temporary branding by way of permanent marker along their right hand.

As Cora's line slowed at the next set of double doors, she turned to see her only friend in the world. Six feet away, and on the wrong side of the inch-thick glass, Trish moved to the front of the line and waited as they scanned her forehead.

Cora's line was again on the move as the masked man in yellow held up the digital readout for his next in command. Both men looked around the massively overcrowded room as another row of women pushed inside. They nodded to one another and as the first man lifted Trish's hand and quickly scribbled out his conclusion, he pointed toward the door nearest Cora's group.

As Trish moved out of line, held her hand up, and started for the door, Cora began to sweat.

One-hundred-one degrees. "*Trish, what the hell did they do to you?*"

4

It definitely wasn't a bar fight. Hell, it really wasn't much of a fight at all. It wasn't a brawl or a skirmish. Neither would anyone confuse what happened before the sun came up as anything resembling an altercation. Griffin Ford laid stretched out across the third row seat and was having trouble even recalling exactly what happened.

Aggressive avoidance, yeah that's it. If he absolutely had to put a label to it, that would be the one. He couldn't remember exactly how the whole thing got started as he was the last to leave the diner, however that man was headed for trouble long before he ran across Griffin and his new co-workers. This was undeniable.

The events that took place shortly after five in the morning still had the SUV buzzing with half-truths and foggy details. Each of the four men had a slightly different interpretation of what took place and also what the bewildered man's motivations actually were. Through the varied stories, one thing remained constant—had the police sirens come even five minutes later, they would have killed that man.

"Okay," Griffin said, to no one in particular, "we all get that he was crazy, or homeless, or whatever. But you've got to give it to the poor guy, his determination was something they write books about."

The man in the passenger seat turned to face the others. "I hit him square in the chest with that two-by-four and he didn't even look like he felt it. That's when I thought we may actually have to kill this dude."

The driver, with thick rows of perspiration now forming along his brow and above his upper lip, turned to the passenger, but didn't speak. He blinked a few times, but didn't join in the conversation. Before turning back to the winding highway, he smiled and tightened his grip on the steering wheel.

The last man, seated along the middle row, noticed the odd exchange and turned back to Griffin. "What's with him?"

Whispering, Griffin said, "Not sure. But he was the first to tangle with that guy, and he did take him to the pavement, I think more than once. Maybe he thinks we should have went easier on that dude. I don't know."

The driver, who was only known to Griffin as Joe M. took his right hand off the wheel, held it skyward, and extended his middle finger. He said nothing to the men, but began to cough. Joe's body convulsed as waves of uncontrollable tremors forced themselves up through into his throat and out through his mouth.

Given that the sun had yet to make its way into their world, the four lane mountain road they traveled remained mostly empty. It had been more than ten minutes since Joe had cut off his high-beams as a courtesy to the passing delivery truck. As he continued to succumb to his involuntary coughing fit, the others took notice when Joe crossed the double yellow line for a second time.

"Hey," Griffin said, "get it together my man, or at least let me drive."

Through his next coughing fit, Joe again saluted the men with his right hand.

Swerving back into the right lane, Joe lowered the driver's window and spat into the pulsing wind.

"Joe, pull it over." Griffin's sat up and leaned into the second row. "We're way ahead of schedule. There's no need to take any chances."

Joe shook his head as the convulsions began to subside. He again held his right hand in the air, this time extending his index finger and calling for the others to give him a minute to compose himself.

Gaining speed as the SUV charged down the next descent, Joe cleared his throat and said, "I'm good, y'all, it's just that breakfast comin' back around on me. That's all."

The man in the passenger seat shook his head and laughed. "You look like ten miles of bad highway, Joe. Your face is the same color grey as your jacket and what's with all the sweat? I've known people in a sauna to perspire less. I think Griffin might be right. Why don't you let one of us drive?"

"Really," Joe said. "Why don't you mind your own business; you know kind of like when you decided to let the rest of us handle that vagrant back in the parking lot."

"I didn't leave. I mean, I just really didn't know what to—"

Griffin interrupted, "Admit it, that guy scared you, didn't he? I'm sure if I'd gotten any closer, I would have run too." Nodding his head, he started to smile. "It's nothing to be ashamed of, just admit it— you left us there to fend for ourselves."

"Yeah right, you have no idea what you're talking about," said the man in the passenger's seat. "You were just coming through the doors when Joe tossed that guy into the dumpster. You missed the entire thing."

Griffin again nodded. "True, but someone had to pick up the tab. You degenerates left the booth before I even had a chance to look up."

"You're the new guy Griffin, and the new guy always—"

"I've known the three of you for less than forty-eight hours, but I can already tell you're all gonna be a pain in my ass... one question though. How did Joe manage to toss that guy into the dumpster on his own? He had to weigh at least two-hundred pounds."

"He had help," said the man in the second row. "That dude came stumbling in through the front doors and right away grabbed at Joe's face. When Joe turned and pushed him backward, out onto the walkway—that guy slammed his head on the concrete. He slammed it real good. We were all surprised when he got back up on his own."

"Then the manager came out?" Griffin said.

"Yeah, I guess he'd been bugging some other people in the parking lot. He just kept coming, really drunk. He even tried to bite Joe's face."

"What?" the man in the passenger seat asked.

"Yeah, that's when we came over. He just kept coming back after Joe. We'd push him away and he'd just get up and come back. He never said a word to us."

"So, you tossed the poor drunk bastard into the dumpster?"

"Yep," Joe said. "I grabbed his arms and he grabbed his legs. We shoved him inside and then watched him try to climb out. It was actually kind of sad. When he wakes up tomorrow—" Joe was cut short as he again started to cough.

Shoving his right foot down on the brake and leaning out, Joe vomited out a mouthful of blood, the other men wincing as it blew back and covered the driver's side of the SUV. Finally, careening into the opposite lane, the SUV slowly came to a stop.

"Joe, get in the back," Griffin said. "You're done."

Joe nodded. "Yeah, whatever."

"I'll drive," Griffin said as he began moving toward the second row. "You get in the passenger seat and give me directions to the building. I don't really care how you feel, we're getting this done today. You can take a sick day tomorrow, once we've all gone our separate ways."

Joe pushed open the driver's door before turning back to Griffin and the others. "Just don't forget who put this thing together. It was my information that led us here. My contacts. My idea. No one else. You're all here because of me."

"Joe, you need to—"

"Don't tell me what I need, I'm giving you more money than you'll see in ten lifetimes. And for what, a few hours of doing what you'd do for free?" Now looking directly at Griffin, he continued, "You got it?"

"Hey, I'm extremely grateful for you letting me in on this job. I just want to get us there in one piece. So let's agree that it's in everyone's best interest for someone else to get behind the wheel."

"Eighteen million dollars," Joe said. "Yes, I know how careful we need to be. I also know that I'm taking the biggest risk. When my brother-in-law finds out that its gone, he'll be looking for me. Only me."

"I thought he and your sister split before the actual wedding?"

"Why do you think we're doing this? My sister is every bit as malicious as the rest of us, she just carries it better. This is her little payback for all his cheating. She's the real reason this is happening. That poor bastard won't even know what or who hit him until I've dug my toes into the sand—" With the others looking on, Joe was hit mid-sentence with another coughing fit and before they could react, he fell face-first onto the asphalt.

Griffin and the man from the passenger seat quickly exited the SUV, made their way over to Joe, and dragged his limp body up onto the rear seat. Two quick slaps from Griffin and a small trail of blood ran from the corner of Joe's mouth. "Come on, wake up."

Nothing.

"JOE, LET'S GO BUDDY!"

No movement.

The man from the passenger seat stepped away as he stared down at his chest, arms, and hands. Slowly walking out to the middle of the roadway, he stood illuminated by the SUV's headlights. "Griffin, who exactly does all this blood belong to?"

5

Was the pounding in his head drowning out the thunder coming from beyond his bedroom or was it the other way around? With the amount of alcohol he'd poured into his six foot-two inch, one-hundred-ninety-five pound body last night, the new day came as a colossal slap in the face. Ethan Runner was sure of four things. He knew he'd gotten less than three hours of sleep. He knew the sun was up. He knew who was pounding at his door. And mostly he knew this day was going to kick his ass.

Sliding out from under the comforter, Ethan pushed into a seated position, rubbed his eyes, and started toward the maniac nearly breaking down his front door. For the third time in as many weeks, his overly enthusiastic best friend and co-worker decided to play good cop.

Crossing the living room, the head-splitting reverberation against the front door began to fade; however, the team of jackhammers working the inside of his forehead amplified their fury. "I'm getting way too old for this—never again."

At the door, he didn't bother to check, as he knew

who it was and why he was here. Stepping aside, he pulled the door open, turned, and started back to the kitchen. "I know, we're late. I just need to dump some caffeine down my throat and after I find my pants, we'll get moving."

David walked through the door as if his heels were on fire. "Hey, I got you covered." His friend followed him away from the entry and held at arm's length a tall cup of the strong stuff. "You got like two minutes to get this stuff in you; we need to go. But I don't care how late we are today, you need a shower. We're not doing this again."

As Ethan moved out of the kitchen, he attempted a compromise. "You know I really don't care about this job, but I don't want you taking the fall for this. Go get the truck and meet me back here in ten minutes, no use in both of us getting the call. Does that work for ya?"

The throbbing behind Ethan's eyes began to manifest itself into a permanent scowl as David fought to keep from laughing. "You know she won't call me and if she reaches the truck she'll want to talk to you anyway. Your sister is relentless."

"Yeah, Emma called me like three times in the middle of the night."

"She what?"

"Probably just trying to make sure I knew what today was."

"You didn't answer?" David said.

"You really think that would have put her mind at ease, hearing me unable to form a complete sentence? I just feel lucky to be alive today. Oh, and by the way, your ability to bounce back after last night is a bit annoying. We consumed the exact same drinks and somehow you seem to have come out the other side without a scratch. You really aren't human, are you?"

David moved to the couch, flopped back into the oversized pillows, and grabbed the TV remote. "Buddy, I stopped drinking hours before you last night. And I hate to say it, but I told you this would happen."

"First of all, nobody likes a know-it-all—it's not funny, it's not clever, and it kinda pisses people off. Oh yeah and while we're at it, NOBODY likes a know-it-all, period."

Before Ethan could finish, David had turned his attention to the television. "Just get in the shower, I'll be the guy on the couch just waiting for you to get your crap together. Now go."

Down the hall and into his bathroom, Ethan turned on the shower and made his way back into his room. "*Where the hell did I leave my phone?*"

Sliding his comforter off the bed and tossing his pillows aside, Ethan tipped the cup back and took another long sip. He quickly scanned the floor and the window ledge. The TV stand was also not the answer. Setting the coffee on the dresser, he crawled across the bed and over to the nightstand, getting brief glimpses of the last six hours.

Steam began to pour out of the bathroom as Ethan found his phone and separated it from the charger. Rolling onto his back and depressing the home button, he glanced back behind the nightstand. Noticing the charger was never plugged into the wall, he tossed his phone onto the bed and hurried into the wall of steam now engulfing the left half of his bedroom. "Five minutes."

Finishing the too hot cup of liquid adrenaline, Ethan quickly moved to the sink, brushed his teeth, and stepped into the shower. Shampoo. Conditioner. Soap. Hot water. The combination had him leaning back against the tile and fighting to keep his eyes open.

He could step out, dry off, and head out the door. He could be twenty to thirty minutes late and then apologize to his sister for once again not living up to the recommendation she'd given him. He could plead with her to not report his fourth tardy this month to their employer and hope they never found out. He could do the right thing. Or he could close his eyes... just for a moment.

·   ·   ·

The water was now running lukewarm. His legs had begun to cramp from the awkward position he found himself in, leaning against the back wall of his shower, and to save his life, Ethan couldn't say how long he'd been asleep. Was it five minutes or two hours. He was fairly certain it wasn't more than a few minutes, as he hadn't heard a word from the living room since David began flipping through the three-hundred channels his satellite dish offered up.

Standing and stretching away the aches of each individual vertebra, Ethan shut off the water and pulled back the curtain. "Dave?"

Nothing

"Hey bud, let me throw on my uniform and we'll get out of here."

Again silence from the adjoining room.

Across his bedroom, Ethan avoided looking out into the rest of the apartment and instead made a beeline for the closet. His powder blue shirts and navy pants lay in three separate piles. One for each day of the week—somehow they were unable to see their way into the hamper.

Down on his knees, the stench emanating from the pile to his right appeared, for the moment, to be the least offensive. Digging free a pair of black socks, he pulled on the heinous poly-blend security uniform, grabbed his Forced Entry, black six-inch Tactical Boots, and strode quickly into the living room. "You ready?"

David didn't hear Ethan, there was something else possessing his attention on the illuminated box ten feet away. He hadn't yet noticed that his friend walked into the room, much less the fact that his shower ended minutes ago. He was no longer in a hurry to get out the door as he flipped from one channel to the next.

Standing at the hall closet, retrieving his firearm, belt, and vest, Ethan stopped to peer over David's shoulder. People running. Chasing one another. Fighting. Attacking. Broken windows. Flames shooting from cars and street level businesses. "What the hell are you watching?"

No response.

Kicking the back of the couch Ethan yelled, "DAVID."

His friend did not turn away from the television, he instead waved Ethan over. "You need to see this."

"I am seeing it, but what is this? People rioting? And where is that, New York?"

David nodded. "Yeah, New York, Chicago, Miami, and Houston, but it looks like the West Coast is getting the worst of it. Whatever this is, I mean they don't really know what it is, but people are losing their minds— they're killing each other for no reason."

"Who?"

"Everyone, I don't know. I don't think anyone knows."

Ethan moved to the window. "What are the local stations saying?"

"Nothing."

"Whatta ya mean?"

"They're all off the air."

6

The doors to the bus parted as the last of the guards and the men in hazmat suits filed out of the building. They weren't quite running, but their hurried pace drew the attention of the twenty-five women. Cora turned to Trish as the last few trickled out into the parking lot. "Trish, what's happening, why are they—"

"Just get on the bus and stay as close to the front as you can."

"Why aren't they telling us anything? I asked why we were being moved and all they'd tell me is that this place isn't safe. But why, why isn't it safe?"

"It doesn't matter," Trish said. "Just get on the bus and keep your eyes open."

"For what, why won't you tell me what happened? I know that you know why they're doing this. I thought we were friends, don't you think—"

"Listen, the less you know about this, the better. No one really knows for sure what this thing is anyway, so they'd just be guessing."

"This thing?"

"Alright," Trish said. "People are getting sick, like

really crazy sick. It started with those newbs they brought in last night. Three of them had these really high fevers, like something that should have killed them."

"What?"

"Yeah, the nursing staff was trying to make them comfortable and give them something for the fever, but they were going nuts. They started attacking the nurses and each other. I was on my last rounds when a few of them came through the door and into the hall. They started coming after me."

"This doesn't make any sense. What did you do?"

"What I always do. I took the first one to the ground and held her there until the guards came and took her away. The second one jumped on my back and the guards took care of her. I got a few bumps and bruises in the process, but I'll be fine."

"So," Cora said. "They're taking us and putting us on buses because a few people are sick? That doesn't make any sense. Why not just get some doctors in here and take care of them?"

Trish pointed to the men at the doors of the bus, now removing their yellow suits and said, "See those guys?"

"Yeah."

"Those men are the only reason you and I are able to get on this bus. They're not doctors, but we are way past that point anyway. I heard them talking and this thing is way bigger than just this place. These sick people are everywhere, so just get on the bus and thank God they didn't lock you in your cell."

"Where are they taking us?"

"At this point, it doesn't really matter."

A male's voice from just beyond the front of the line called for attention. "Listen up ladies. Nothing has changed. You will get on, take a seat where we tell you, and you will shut your mouths. If anyone has a problem with that, you are welcome to stay here, but I wouldn't recommend it." He paused briefly, stepped out away from the bus, glaring up and down the line. "Anybody have a problem?"

No one spoke

"Good."

The four mystery men, followed by the six female guards, boarded first. They nodded to the driver, another rough looking older gentleman, as they moved up the two steps and into the aisle. The men took the first two rows and the guards filed in behind, with only two taking a seat at the rear of the bus.

As the line began to move, Cora looked back at the main building and over at Trish. "Here we go."

"Remember what I said, you need to take a seat as close to the front as you can. When we stop, you get off as quick as you can. Don't wait for me."

"Wait for you?"

Trish stiffened. "I'm going to the back of the bus. I don't have a choice. They're saying my temperature is borderline. And—"

"And?"

"It could be nothing, but they aren't taking any chances. They said I could stay here or sit in the back. You already know what I chose."

The line again moved forward and Cora reached back, grabbing Trish's hand. It was warm and moist to the touch. She smiled nervously as they stepped onto the bus and took a seat behind the three rows of guards, noticing her friend wince as the two parted. Looking down at her hand, Cora was left with fragments of dried blood she assumed somehow belonged to her best friend.

The guard to her right, attempting to get a head count, motioned toward the right side of the aisle. "Adams, take a seat."

Figuring the current circumstances may afford her the opportunity to dig a bit deeper, Cora allowed the woman if front of her to slide in and she took the seat facing out. Addressing the guard, she said, "What's going on? You guys aren't telling us any—"

"No questions, just sit there and keep your mouth shut."

"But, you haven't—"

"I'll tell you what, you want some answers? Get the hell off my bus, go back across that parking lot, and check it out for yourself? I guarantee you'll wish you stayed in that seat."

"Thanks," Cora said. "That clears things up."

The guard shook her head and turned back to her head count as the last few women moved into their seats. "Ms. Adams, don't forget your place. I won't tell you again."

As the bus shifted into gear and began to pull away from the curb, a few errant gasps pulled Cora's attention back to the facility. The lights in the distance near the yard were the first to blink out, followed in quick succession by the numbered buildings one at a time until the entire sixty acre property sat in darkness. "Huh?"

.   .   .

Unable to remember exactly when she'd fallen asleep, Cora leaned to the side and peered out the front windshield. "Wow." The sun hadn't yet made its appearance, although it lit the morning just enough for her to see that they'd nearly reached the valley. She estimated it was less than an hour since they pulled away, however it felt as if she'd slept for three days.

The small town in the distance sat quiet as the bus sped along the two lane road, rounding one hairpin after another. Tiny lights from the valley below twinkled and then faded out as they moved from one grouping of trees to the next. Cora twisted in her seat and attempted eye contact with her friend, only to be blocked by two of the larger men.

They appeared to be struggling with one of the more unruly passengers, although Cora couldn't get a glimpse of exactly who it was. "*Better them than me.*"

Before rounding the next turn, Cora turned back around. Partially hidden through the muted morning light, a blacked-out SUV sat less than one hundred feet away, and positioned along the middle of the road, its headlights stared back.

Instinctively sliding down in her seat and pulling

her legs to her chest, Cora closed her eyes. Placing her head between her knees, she took a deep breath and braced for impact. "*Please, please, please.*"

7

Out the front doors of his building and into the street, it was surprisingly quiet for this time of the morning. Other than the single alarm sounding from somewhere at the other end of town, you'd think the entire city was dead. According to David, they were more than thirty minutes behind schedule; however, as Ethan reminded his friend, "This wasn't something that a few shortcuts through town couldn't fix."

"Yeah," David said, "I'm sure your sister will absolutely feel the same way."

"Emma will be fine, she always is."

"That's all good and everything and you may be cool with being one write up away from the unemployment line, but I need this job. I mean I'm completely grateful for you hooking me up, but I really do need this."

"No worries, I'll just call... damn it!"

"What now?" David said.

"I forgot my phone, but it really wouldn't have mattered anyway; the battery was dead before I even fell asleep last night."

"Let's just get to the truck and you can use mine to call her."

"Can't."

"Why?"

"I don't know her number," Ethan said. "It's in my phone, but I can't remember the last time I actually had to dial it."

"Great," David said. "So this will *actually* be our last day of work. Oh well, it was nice while it lasted."

Ethan shook his head and continued up the long block toward Old Bridge Road before turning onto Second Street. Reaching the newly constructed building, he walked through the door and hurried up the stairs to the second floor.

Working for the man who employed his sister had its privileges. Directly reporting to her was not one of those perks. He and David were brought on a little over six months before when a large donation was made to their humble city in exchange for the benefactor's anonymity. The company, and more precisely the man behind the company, demanded to remain in the shadows.

.   .   .

Ethan's sister Emma moved back to town for exactly thirty days, to meet with the building commission and the bank manager and to ensure the transition played out exactly as planned. She was also assigned the responsibility of reporting back on the construction of the two adjoining structures.

First City Bank more than doubled its square

footage and for the first time, owned a vault that would accommodate more than two people at a time. The building attached to the bank's west wall, and also built by the mystery investor, offered only one office and a reception desk that sat along the expansive second floor. The first floor was nothing more than a few potted plants and three severely uncomfortable leather chairs.

Only days before his sister's arrival, she proposed a plan to pull Ethan out of his yearlong depression. She offered him one of only three jobs within this small satellite office. He would drive an armored truck from the lot behind the bank into the city, load into the armored vehicle whatever he was asked, and without making a single stop, he'd deliver the load back to the bank and then be done for the day.

As Ethan reluctantly agreed to take the job, he had one request. He asked that Emma also bring on his best friend and pay him twice what he was making. He knew David wanted to start a family and presumed that the man in charge of this operation had unlimited resources. Their meager salaries would be of little concern to a company worth millions.

Emma agreed without a second thought. She set them up with uniforms, two armored vehicles (one black and one white) to be driven on alternate days, and three weeks of basic weapons training. The day she said goodbye, she handed them each a new utility belt, an Austrian born Glock 17, and a "Welcome to BXF Technologies" handbook.

The uniforms were fine—at least he wouldn't have to worry about choosing what to wear every day and for Ethan, driving the massive vehicles was as much fun as one could have while still getting paid. Also, never having to worry about some of the more serious traffic infractions had its appeal, within reason.

His sister explained that he must do whatever he had to do to get his route completed by five in the afternoon. This must happen each and every shift, without exception. If he and David had to work through their lunch, then so be it. If they had to start earlier in the morning, that was okay too. If they needed to avoid pausing at every single stop sign, she wouldn't ask them any questions. If there were any problems, she promised to personally have them taken care of. Ethan just needed to make sure he got his job done. Every. Single. Day.

Ethan was in no position to decline the job offer, even though that's exactly what his gut told him to do. Over the last six months, he'd given his sister more than enough reasons to find someone else— anyone else for the position. His sights were elsewhere and everyone could see it.

Three days before she arrived in town, the siblings spoke on the phone for over two hours. He later told her that if he'd known what she was calling about, he would have never taken her call. She told him that she'd do most of the talking and that this was one conversation where he really needed to listen, even if he didn't want to. "Ethan—Mom, Dad, and I have waited long enough for you to bounce back. But now we need you to meet us halfway. We love you and are worried about you. This is as good an opportunity as you're going to get."

. . .

Ethan's life collapsed the day his fiancée left town. There was no warning, no goodbyes, and no time for him to come to terms with the loss. The two never spoke again and as he attempted to put the pieces back together, his upcoming position as deputy sheriff was eliminated due to budget constraints.

As the days turned to weeks and he continued to freefall into depression, Ethan received a phone call that would forever change his life. He was told that his father had suffered a heart attack coming down the mountain and had completely lost control of his truck. The tree he plowed into was older than the valley itself, and after eight hours of intensive surgery, he received the first bit of good news in over a year. His father would live.

Exactly sixty-one days later, the final two blows were handed down, each more devastating than the one before.

His father needed to move closer to where his rehab facility was located, in the city. The drive back and forth, three times per week, was doing as much damage to his mother's health as it was healing his father. This would mean he'd only see them every other weekend; however, with as much as he'd lost in the last year, he still had his sister. And the very next day, that was also taken away.

After more than six years of working to complete her bioengineering degree, and then flying around the country for interviews, Emma received the job offer of a lifetime. A company with deeply rooted ties to the military and government demanded that she join their team out on the West Coast within the month. She couldn't say no.

Her conversation with Ethan went as well as could be expected. What she couldn't foresee was how much further he'd sink in the coming months. They spoke nearly every single day and she came back to town as often as she could manage. It was never enough, not for her and definitely not for him.

.   .   .

The day Emma returned to officially offer him the job, her brother appeared older. Not his physical appearance, but the way he carried himself. His outward demeanor. He was friendly, he finally laughed again. He was having fun with life, and many nights too much fun. Life had beaten down the thirty-eight-year-old man who she grew up idolizing, but for the first time in a long time, Ethan looked happy.

He was softened by the things that kicked and punched him, but he was a man. He looked at things with a much different eye now, but knew what he wanted and initially that didn't include a job driving a truck full of someone else's money.

He agreed to do what his sister asked, but only

until the sheriff's office had another position available. The experience he gained through this opportunity may just look good on a resume, even if he had to list his sister as his supervisor.

8

Dropping out of the sky as the sun began its forward push along the West Coast, the unnerving turbulence pulled Emma from the fitful nap she'd succumbed to less than an hour earlier. As her eyes adjusted to the dimly lit rear cabin, she straightened in her seat, brushed her hair from her face, and glanced the two side tables.

As her world crystalized, she reached for her phone, entered her password, and noticed the lack of reception the plane's interior offered. "Great."

As the jet banked right, the first hint of what was to come appeared through the window on the opposite side of the plane. Not more than a few miles from where they were to touch down, the city streets were a virtual war zone. From an altitude of less than three-thousand feet, spot fires peppered the urban landscape, only to be eclipsed by the countless number of vehicles attempting to flee the area.

As the Gulfstream continued its descent, Emma stretched the exhaustion from her back, legs, and arms. With one hand braced against the right wall, she stood and started for the cockpit. Moving past the stainless-steel-trimmed appliance stack, and dual coffee makers, she was greeted by the flight's Private Concierge.

He was good looking, but not intimidating. He smiled, although only enough to make certain he had her full attention. His voice came out of the dimly lit galley in a calm and professional tone. He slid closed the cockpit privacy divider and held out his hand as Emma approached. "Ms. Runner, is there something I can get for you? We are actually about to land."

"Have the pilots seen what is happening out there?"

"Yes, we are all very aware of the situation. We've been re-routed to Burbank and have a car waiting for you."

"Have you spoken to Mr. Goodwin? He's going to want to know—"

"Yes Ms. Runner, he's instructed us to get you to your destination and wait for our next assignment."

"Next assignment? It looks like Armageddon down there. Why don't we just fly somewhere else?"

"Well, there isn't anywhere else. Burbank is the only alternative, the only one still taking flights, aside from LAX."

"Okay, then why not LAX? It would be closer from there to my house anyway."

"Yes it would be much closer, although as you can see, the streets are impassable from there into Inglewood or even Playa Del Ray. Nearly everything heading north is going to be a no go. It's Burbank. Only Burbank."

Attempting to look out the left window, Emma leaned forward. "What about Mr. Goodwin? Isn't he flying into LAX? He said that he and Mr. Dalton were heading back to the offices, aren't they going to be heading right into—"

"They took a different route and landed nearly thirty minutes ago. Mr. Goodwin is already into the city and should be arriving safely at the building in just a few minutes. He wanted to pass along his well-wishes and asked that we get you to your destination quickly and safely."

Well-wishes? Emma thought. *Sounds like he's sending a Christmas card.* "Did he give any details as to what—"

The privacy door to the cockpit slid open and the co-pilot leaned out through the opening. He nodded to the Concierge and disappeared back behind the controls of the G280.

"Ms. Runner, we're landing. You'll need to take your seat."

She paused for a moment longer, but only stared. He was kind and composed and would certainly give an answer to anything she asked. It was just that the questions she had couldn't be answered by this concierge only minutes before they touched down and she knew it. Emma smiled and before turning away simply said, "Thank you."

Moving through the rear cabin, she avoided the windows and instead reached for her phone. Sliding back into her seat, she again opened her messages. Three new texts, all from Marcus Goodwin. Before viewing the most recent, she opened the one sided conversation sent to her brother.

Reading back through her unanswered texts, she shook her head before adding one last request. *Ethan, I'm heading home. Please get back with me as soon as you can.*

As the text struggled to send through the poor signal, she opened the message from Goodwin. *Emma, I need the documentation from the most recent test subjects uploaded to my private server as soon as you get home. And, be sure to use the VPN from your desktop ONLY.*

The second message was time stamped only seconds after the first. *Emma, Our mainframe appears to be experiencing some delays, go ahead and let the upload continue for as long as it takes. I need those results this morning.*

The last was send only minutes before she opened her phone. *You should be landing in the next few minutes. A car will be waiting at the hanger when you arrive. You will be home no later than seven-thirty. I'll be expecting the report by eight.*

Shaking her head, Emma leaned forward and pulled her bag in between her feet. Opening the side pocket, she dropped her phone in, just as it began to ring.

9

Snow began to fall as Griffin stepped away from the rear door of the SUV. The intermittent winds pushing in through the lower elevations sent reams of white powder from the elevated tree line out onto the roadway. The light dusting filtered in through the opened rear doors, clinging to the SUV and blurring the lines between where the asphalt ended and the forest began.

Calling out for the man from the passenger seat, his arms started to cramp and his lungs were on fire. Performing CPR on the man who face-planted out on the roadway wasn't working. The third man continued his efforts from the rear seat as Griffin shouted across the vehicle. "He's not responding."

"What do we do?"

"He needs to get to a hospital," Griffin said. "But, it's probably already too late."

"This doesn't look good, we gotta get out of here. Let's go back to that town."

"And what? Just leave him in the car, out in front of the hospital and then catch the next bus out of town?"

"You got a better plan?"

Looking back into the SUV, Griffin shook his head. "I don't know, but we do need to get the hell out of here." Stepping to the driver's door, he said, "Where are the keys?"

"Try Joe's pockets."

The man from the second row stepped out of the SUV and waved the others over. "Uh, there's something you guys need to see. It's Joe."

"Did you get him breathing?" Griffin said.

"No, that's not it. He's got a pretty good gash on his right arm. It looks like he was bitten."

"So?"

"I don't know, it just looks weird and he's lost a lot of blood. Do you think that homeless guy bit him?"

Turning back to the SUV, the light reflecting off the chrome mirrors preceded the sound of tires gripping the roadway by only a fraction of a second. Instinctively diving into the thick underbrush at the side of the road, Griffin managed only a brief glimpse of the massive collision, and the other two men caught between the transport vehicle and the SUV.

The man from the passenger seat was the first hit. He was unaware of the approaching bus and was still walking back to the SUV when he was struck. Clipped by the left front bumper, he was thrown nearly thirty feet.

Floating away amongst the falling snowflakes, Griffin lost sight of the man's body as it twisted violently around a massive sequoia and then dropped to the undergrowth below. The image and sound were distorted as the bus came into full view and struck the last man.

Momentarily pinned between the front bumpers of both vehicles, the man's body and facial expression went slack. As the SUV went airborne and separated momentarily from the bus, the body dropped to the pavement and slid face-first to the opposite side of the road.

Griffin scrambled to his feet as the bus began to drift to the right after the collision. It was thrown onto its side and showed no signs of slowing as it moved toward him and the dense patch of trees at his back. Sparks rose from the right and left sides, as it appeared to gain momentum sliding downhill across the snow dusted asphalt.

The slope he came to rest on was blocked in on three sides. The only way to avoid having the gargantuan bus drift off the highway and directly into him was to go toward it. Scaling the short ascent, he begged his legs for more.

As it sunk in that he would be unable to completely clear the scene, Griffin took two more steps forward and turned his back on the charging giant. He wrapped his arms around his head and braced for a direct hit.

Brilliant flashes of white lightning shot across his eyes as he went airborne. Shockwaves of agony traveled from his hips up into the base of his neck and then back down to his feet as he tumbled head over heels between the trunks of two large trees. On his back and sliding to a stop in the thick underbrush, he listened for his own heartbeat.

The world went silent as Griffin came to rest ten feet beyond the windshield of the bus. Covered in upturned soil and craning his neck from right to left, the pain running the length of his body appeared to only be superficial. Pulling his legs toward his chest and rounding his shoulders, he took in a deep breath. "So, I'm still here, I just hope that's a good thing."

Pushing up onto his feet, he ran his hands up and down his legs and over his torso. Other than the feeling that every nerve ending covering his six-foot frame had been lit on fire, he appeared to have avoided any serious damage. He could walk and for the moment had full use of his extremities. He was now obligated to help with the chaotic mess just inside the bus at his feet.

Grasping the underside of the wheel-well, Griffin pulled his way up to the hillside in time to see the SUV fully engulfed in flames. As he moved to the opposite end, the blaze began to spread to the bus where the two touched, near the larger vehicle's rear roofline.

Griffin moved quickly between the two men with whom he'd spent the last several hours, both having sustained fatal injuries when thrown from the roadway. Still unable to completely understand this situation or how he got here, he took a full trip around both vehicles, searching for a spot to climb onto the bus and get to those who had begun to scream for help.

Back to the front end, Griffin was left with only one option. Running back toward the SUV, he searched the forest floor and came away with the base of the tire jack. Having to slide Joe's body aside, a chill tore through his body as he paused and imagined the grotesquely deformed man's eyes opening.

Back to the bus's windshield, Griffin stepped to the side and hoisted the thirty pound jack overhead. Arching back and then leaning in, he catapulted the awkwardly heavy metal object at the corner of the already cracked glass.

The windshield splintered into a thousand pieces and crumbled onto the passenger compartment. Reaching in, he retrieved the jack and slid it out of the way. His hand on the steering wheel, Griffin squatted down and gazed into the wrecked interior. As the cries for help and the flames grew at the rear of the bus, Griffin stepped inside. "I'm gonna need some help."

10

The only other resident employed by BXF Technologies was Shannon. Her job title was receptionist, but Ethan suspected she was much, much more. She was courteous, but deeply private. Most days she wore a fire engine red blouse and jet black polyester slacks. She lived on the opposite side of town and was never seen out of her home after sunset. Considerate and attractive, she was also agonizingly professional.

She offered Ethan and David a greeting each and every morning, and not much conversation beyond that. She showed up at eight in the morning, every morning. She promptly shut down her computer at five in the afternoon and rarely if ever left the building. You could set your clock by this woman. But not today. Today at exactly nine-fifteen the second floor, and more importantly her desk, sat vacant.

David shoved Ethan forward at the top of the stairs and moved to the office in the corner. "So? Where's your girl?"

"My girl?"

"Yeah," David said. "There is no way you can tell me you don't have a thing for that woman. I've known you way too long and have seen the way you look at her."

"You need to get your eyes checked then, she has no interest in the opposite sex. And she especially has no interest in me, anyone can see that."

David moved to the desk that sat ten feet from the floor-to-ceiling, plate-glass windows overlooking the majority of the city. "I didn't say she was into you, she would have to be out of her mind to have anything to do with a bum like you. But you're pretty transparent. I don't think I've seen you go more than five minutes without staring at her."

"Yeah, she's an attractive woman, but I'm not really looking for—"

Now seated at the computer, David finished logging their run. "Hey, were you able to get to your email last night before we left?"

"Yeah, just a few from Emma. She was in New York meeting with you know who. She was originally going to come through this weekend, but wanted to avoid those insane chili cook-off fanatics."

"You know what's weird, I didn't see any of them out this morning. I know a few of them had the same kind of night we did, but usually they're out setting up by now. You remember last year don't you?"

Ethan moved away from the desk and over to the window overlooking Second Street. "Yeah, I remember not being able to leave my apartment for two days. Those chili-heads were everywhere. I walked more that weekend than in my entire life. It was hell."

"Okay," David said. "Then where the hell is everyone? The streets are empty and the fact that Shannon's not here is a bit disturbing."

Ethan laughed. "I love that you seem just as put off by Shannon not being here as you are by the entire city looking like a ghost town. You are too good for words."

"Let me ask you this," David said. "Has she ever been one minute late? Has she ever called in sick? Has that women ever even taken one day off since we started?"

"I don't really—"

"We're back up, the Wi-Fi seems to be working, and you have three emails from Emma, all before six this morning. And all of them marked urgent."

"Oh boy, what's it this time? Another double-run today?"

"Not quite. It's the same three messages. Just worded differently. It looks like she just really needs to talk to you. She wants you to call her ASAP."

"Hey," Ethan said. "Don't we have her on speed dial on the house phone?"

David slid the phone across the desk, closed his email, and opened a browser window, first checking the local forecast. "We're gonna get some snow today. Should be fine. You able to get Emma on the phone?"

Shaking his head, Ethan said, "Nope, lines are dead. Let's just get this run out of the way and I'll call her from my phone later."

"You sure? Sounds like she really needs to talk to you. I don't think I've ever seen her send an email marked urgent."

"Yeah, I'm sure she's just looking to give me crap about being late. And by the time I call her, hopefully she will have calmed down, so it's a win-win. Let's go."

David couldn't erase what he'd seen earlier at Ethan's apartment and even if it was on the other side of the country, he wanted more information. Heading to the various news sites he frequented, the images along the front page were alarming. "Ethan, you need to see this."

Ethan moved from the opposite side of the desk and slid in beside his friend. "See what?"

"That stuff from the news, it's everywhere."

People, who otherwise appeared normal attacked one another, almost as if possessed. From the awkward angles of a majority of the shots, most taken from a distance, these individuals moved like animals. The aggressors pursued their prey without reason or a sense of self-preservation. As David flipped through the major video sharing sites, new clips were uploaded faster than he could view them. "What the hell is going on?"

"Click that one on the right, titled... *Feeders.*"

As the video began, the first few seconds jumped around like a marble in a coffee can. Nothing on the screen could be seen for more than a millisecond. Obviously someone running, every desperate breath more pronounced than the one before. As it hit the twenty second mark, the video momentarily went black and then was quickly turned onto its side, the camera pointing directly at the latest victim.

The sound had been muted and the lower third of the frame was occupied by a slow moving river of what looked like charred motor oil. It ran from the massive wound at back of the victim's head and slowly pooled around the camera. As the lens refocused, the image became clear.

Only the top of the aggressors head and shoulders were visible as he moved on his hands and knees into the frame and leaned over his victim's face. Thrusting his head forward and pulling away multiple times, the video paused and then restarted. As the thing that was supposed to be human pulled away, David shot back in his chair. "OH. MY. GOD."

As his friend slid backward, Ethan leaned in. "He just tore off that guy's face, look."

"Yeah, I can see that. But what is it that I am actually seeing. What in the world is wrong with that guy?"

"Drugs?"

"No," David said. "This stuff is happening in too many places. It has to be some sort of a virus—a plague or something. Maybe terrorism, I don't know."

As the video continued to roll and the two friends looked on, the much smaller man on top began to claw at his prey. One repulsive handful of flesh at a time, he pulled the larger man apart. Not satisfied with what he'd seized with his teeth, the crazed individual leaned back and began forcing the blood-soaked shards of skin from his victim's chest and abdomen into his mouth.

As the larger man flailed in agony and then rapidly went still, David paused the video and looked away. "This isn't right, it can't be. Normal people don't act like that."

Scrolling through the images along the right side of the page, David turned to his friend. "Ethan, this one is from the city."

"Okay?"

"What about your parents?"

11

Opening her eyes, Cora was unable to move. Pinned beneath two motionless bodies, her heart began to race as sweat ran from her forehead and dripped onto the woman below. Attempting to scream for help, her words were stopped short. She could breathe, but only in quick short bursts as the weight from above continued to settle.

The bus that had been upright and gliding along the mountain road only minutes ago had become little more than a chaotic mess of arms, legs, and screams of agony. The distant cries were coming from behind and toward the rear of the hollow steel tube she was now trapped inside. "Trish, please be alive."

As the confused shouting at the back of the bus quickly turned to screams for help, Cora slid her hands to her chest. Nearly forgetting her wrists were bound, she pushed off the window at her back and twisted away from the two bodies trapping her against the woman below.

Finally able to take a full breath, Cora pushed backward and wedged herself into a semi-standing position. From her new vantage, she was able to look over the sea of bodies and further on, the fire that had begun to consume the rear of the bus. And although the flames had yet to breach the interior, there wasn't yet cause to celebrate. She was still wearing a pair of standard issue handcuffs. There were countless bodies between her and the exit and as she watched her friend surface ten feet away, smoke had begun to fill the space.

Sliding her hands up, Cora unzipped her coveralls and wiggled out of the lower half. With the bright orange fabric now a tangled mess around her cuffs, she held the damp material over her mouth and nose. Short shallow breaths were still easier for her to manage and turning back toward the chaos at the rear of the bus, Cora found her friend.

Among the mismatched arms, legs, and torsos, Trish clawed her way on top of the pile, only feet from the advancing flames. She pulled at the lifeless victims, moving from one perversely misshapen body to the next. Her head down and fighting for every inch, Trish slowed as the bus rocked under its own weight.

With less than fifteen feet separating the pair, and the desperate voices slowly succumbing to their injuries, the bus grew quiet. Sliding to her left and standing high on her toes, Cora filled her lungs and shouted. "Trish."

What she saw as her friend lifted her head, confused her. As her and the others were rushed from their cells and out into the halls, she'd seen this same look across the few lifeless bodies left out in the open. The thick white haze that covered her friend's eyes. The bewildered, almost animal like quality of her stare. And the blood, unevenly obscuring the edges of her mouth, dripped from her chin as she met Cora's gaze.

"Trish... No. Please. No."

Had Trish been infected by whatever took the others? Was she simply reacting to the accident? What was this and why had it taken some and not others? Back toward the front of the bus, looking for an exit, Cora winced as the bus shifted once again, threatening to pull away from the SUV and down the graduated slope.

Biting at the dead air and tearing at each new corpse she traversed, Trish was gone. What now occupied her body was no longer the women she trusted with her life. The animal that her friend had become struggled to continue forward through the forty-five-foot graveyard, and peering right through Cora's eyes, raised her head and growled.

"Someone help. Please someone, anyone."

Of the thirty-six individuals who had boarded the bus less than an hour before, not one responded. *Had all those that were still alive been crushed beneath the dead and were now unable to speak? Were they simply too afraid? Had the women in the back already been overcome by the smoke and flames? Were they all dead?*

It didn't matter. No one responded and no one was going to help her. Cora would get herself out of this, just like she always did. Just like her father told her she always would. She didn't need anyone, or anything.

Left with only one option—turning and going through the front windshield, she again, out of morbid curiosity, looked back at Trish. Her friend had been caught by the fire that was quickly spreading, although she still progressed toward her.

Both hands reaching for the seatback to her right, the bus again slipped on the icy road, shifting its grisly contents from left to right. Cora awkwardly slid between two guards, one of which had her throat cut by the jagged metal of the caved in roof. Leaning back, she pulled her legs up and placing her feet along the waist of the dead woman, pushed her away.

Through the darkened cabin, shadows played tricks with her eyes. Cora looked from left to right and back again, scanning the guard's belt. She knew the exact placement of the keys she'd need to free herself from the cuffs, although with the obvious trauma the body had taken in the accident, the retractable keyset appeared to now rest somewhere behind the guard's back.

Quickly calculating the time it would take to readjust the guard's position, turn her around, and then fumble to remove the cuffs, Cora looked back at Trish. She didn't have nearly that much time.

The rear of the bus now fully engulfed in the flames that had also advanced on her friend, Cora again repositioned her feet atop the guard's shoulders. She slowly slid up and out of the pile holding her down. Again moving her arms above her head, she reached for the seat on the opposite side of the bus, clutched the tubular railing, and pulled away.

Less than five feet separated the friends as Cora lay atop the mound of bodies flat on her back. Craning her head backward, she was able to see daylight coming through the front of the bus in long slivers. Back through her legs, she was only able to see her friend's face, arm, and shoulders as Trish continued toward her.

The bruises, lacerations, and removal of large swatches of skin along her friend's wrists spoke of how Trish had been able to climb out of her spot at the rear of the bus and advance nearly thirty feet in under two minutes. Her badly malformed fingers and hands were evidence of the pain involved. Boarding the bus, every single woman who wasn't a guard wore a pair of shiny silver bracelets meant to induce compliance. Trish had pulled hers off.

Tears formed at the corners of Cora's eyes and began to roll down the sides of her face and into her thick brown hair. As the dense smoke continued to fill the void and filter in around Trish, the flames licked at her back and then quickly ignited her hair. Was she watching her friend die or had that already happened?

The shattering of glass and a rush of cool air preceded the bus once again jerking forward. The pressure difference, along with the bus's movement, shoved Cora down and to the left. As the smoke pushed out through the opening and daylight took its place, a voice came through the shadows.

"Hey, anybody there?"

Trish was now on her. She had Cora's left ankle in her right hand and began to pull.

"Yes, but I need help, like right now."

The entity that was her friend reached out with her left hand, grabbed ahold of Cora's other ankle and gradually inched forward.

"I'm coming, but you're going to have to help."

Cora kicked and tried to push away, although Trish's grip wouldn't be denied. The more she struggled, the further she slid down and to the left.

"I'm on my back and can't move. Can't you come to me?"

Sweat now ran from her face and neck, pooling at her back and down into her waist. The radiant heat moving from the rear of the bus seemed to intensify as it fought the cool air pushing in from behind.

"Okay, but it may take me a few minutes. How many are there that need help?"

She couldn't tell if Trish was coming toward her or if she was being pulled back. Judging by the heat and the flames that had completely overtaken her friend, she'd have guessed the latter.

"I'm not sure, I can't see anyone else, but I don't have another two minutes—I don't even think I have another thirty seconds."

The bus shifted again and this time it tossed Cora out of the pocket she was in, and deposited her alongside her friend. Now less than eighteen inches apart, Trish moved in and began frantically clawing at her as she shielded her face with her hands, the only protection provided by the thin coveralls wrapped tightly around her arms.

Cora started to shake as Trish climbed on top, leaned in, and bared her teeth. A coagulated mess of blood and saliva slipped from the corners of her mouth and fell onto Cora's bare neck. Daring to meet her friends gaze, she followed the trail of blood to Trish's neck and down to her exposed right shoulder. Two distinct sets of teeth marks outlined a large section of missing flesh. Someone or something had bitten her friend, and the same thing was about to happen to her.

"Help, please hurry."

12

Ethan moved back to the window as David's curiosity continued to grow. With his connection to the internet coming and going and the bandwidth slowing to a crawl, he abandoned the video sharing sites and instead started searching forums. He looked for any threads started within the last few hours, regardless of title. From what he could surmise, this was the only thing being discussed online.

Avoiding any of the conspiracy theory forums and opting only for sites that appeared well informed, he found his way to a website that showed nearly one million active members, of which 86,000 were currently online. The first and most active thread was titled '*WTF is happening*'. He didn't have a clue, and it appeared that no one else did either.

As he opened the thread and his connection slowed once again, David turned back to Ethan. "Just give me a few minutes; I want to see what I can find out before we go. You cool with that?"

Only half paying attention, Ethan nodded. "Sure, but I think I found those crazy chili fanatics."

Back to his work, David returned the same level of

enthusiasm. "Yeah, okay." He read the first post and had the same exact question. *What is happening to people? Is this some sort of sickness or mass terrorism?* The first page of more than fifty included little information and was filled mainly with those looking to add to the already out of control hysteria.

One theory told of a super virus that had become airborne and would kill each new host within minutes. Another described a story where the latest round of flu shots had turned its consumers into bloodthirsty vampires. And still another tried to sell the idea of the government infecting its own citizens as a form of population control.

David didn't buy any of these, and neither did anyone else. Glancing through pages ten through twenty brought stories from those actually living the incidents. They told firsthand accounts of what the video sharing sites had portrayed, as most had gone offline due to the server-strangling amount of traffic each site was attempting to manage.

Page eighteen stopped David's search, as he found a lengthy post from a woman in Atlanta who was on her way to the gym with her husband when the madness rolled through. She described a group of six crazed individuals so badly disfigured that she had trouble distinguishing the men from the women.

Stopped at an intersection, they ran across the half dozen out of control individuals as they poured out of the local coffee house in pursuit of a lone female. At first the woman assumed that she and her husband had become involved in an elaborate prank, but quickly understood the severity as those wide-eyed men and women began beating her vehicle with their bare hands.

They approached from the driver's side and tore at her mirrors, pulling free the weather-stripping around the window. As the largest in the group leapt onto the hood, she said her forty-seven-year-old husband stepped out of the passenger side and confronted the six ravenous people.

Before he was able to question those attempting to destroy his vehicle, he was tackled to the ground by the man on the hood. The others moved in quickly as he slid backward and up onto the sidewalk. Giving up on the female who'd sprinted away from the intersection, the riotous animals turned their full attention to her husband.

Continuing the story, the woman told of how she lowered her window and screamed that her husband return to the car. He immediately obliged and narrowly finding his way into the back seat, the woman turned the car around and headed away from the downtown square.

Heading home, the woman said that she noticed an alarming amount of blood running from her husband's right hand and noticed he'd been bitten by the man that had left the hood and chased him down. She tried three different twenty-four hour clinics, only to return home as not one was open that morning for business.

The woman continued to post every few minutes with updates as her husband's condition began to deteriorate. First came the uncontrollable fever and within an hour signs of delirium. As the woman became aware of just how widespread the calamity was, she warned others away from her hometown.

Continuing to scan the next few pages, the woman's posts began to taper off. She indicated that she checked on her husband every few minutes and that he started going in and out of consciousness. He stopped breathing and then again started just before she tried to call for an ambulance. She indicated that the emergency number had rung for over an hour, without anyone picking up.

In her final post, the desperate woman from Atlanta who'd been a member of the forum for less than two months, asked for prayers and said that she was going to the living room to sit with her husband. She would continue dialing for help, although his face had gone flush, and his pulse was slowing with each passing minute. Her last six words... "I fear this is the end."

Before refreshing the page, David paused and looked at the phone. He picked it up, hit the dial button, and held it to his ear. "Damn it." Still no dial tone.

As Ethan turned away from the window, his smile was oddly out of place. Beyond the floor-to-ceiling windows rose a stack of smoke from somewhere along the eastern edge of town. David knew that the dense brown column meant that somewhere a structure was burning.

Nodding to Ethan he said, "I think we need to get

out there and see what's going on, and what's with the smile?"

"Emma's gonna kill me. Those chili people are out past the library and blocking Main, all the way up to Third Street. They're just milling around out there like cattle. We're gonna have to go all the way around and take Fourth back to Main."

"I don't know man, whatever's happening out there looks like it's taking over, taking over everything. It's not just the big cities. It's everywhere. I say we go check Shannon's house, then run by the hospital just to make sure."

"Make sure of what?" Ethan said. "That those things from the internet don't come running through our pitiful little town? Trust me, no one wants to come here, not even those... whatever they are. I mean the people that live here have been trying to escape for years, and—"

"Speak for yourself."

"I always do."

"Okay Mister Know-it-All, so what's with the smoke, and why aren't there any sirens?"

"Well, for one," Ethan said, "I assume that's coming from the super awesome, people magnet that is the Chilifest. You know, out there at John's farm. And there probably aren't any sirens because every fireman within thirty miles is over there waiting to get a taste of all that free chili."

"Either way, we need to get in the truck and do something."

"You mean like, our jobs?"

David shook his head, "You actually wanting to work? Wow, this world must really be coming to an end. That has never happened."

Ethan reached into the desk and grabbed the keys. "There's a first time for everything."

13

Waving the smoke away, Griffin dragged the first three limp bodies he came across to the side of the road before he was able to spot her. The fire that spread from the SUV had now taken over the entire rear of the overturned bus and was quickly advancing.

Leaning in, he brushed aside the largest shards of broken glass and nearly fell back as the driver appeared to move. Squatting, he placed his index and middle finger along the driver's carotid, and continued to find the female voice. "I'm coming, just keep talking, what's your name?"

"Cora, my name is Cora, please help." The intensity in her voice now outpaced the flames consuming the bus. "There's someone back here that's... that's trying to kill me."

Unable to locate a pulse, Griffin slid the driver out of the way, although he was still focused on the unusual facial characteristics of the lifeless older gentleman. With his eyes fixed in a blank stare and the last of his motor impulses used to open and close his jaw, the driver was obviously gone.

Stepping over another badly mangled corpse, Griffin spotted the body that belonged to the voice. Positioned flat on her back, the petite woman fought off the advances of her much larger aggressor.

Moving through the tight space, Griffin was hit with the wall of heat as he reached for an errant bottle of water. Removing the lid, he tossed it end over end at the flaming beast. Now less than six feet separating him from the woman he needed to get to, he noticed her handcuffs and bright orange jumpsuit protecting her from the woman who'd pinned her down.

The bottle of water connecting with its intended target, he shouted. "Hey... you, what are you—"

As the scorched attacker looked up, met his eyes, and began to growl, Griffin stopped. The woman's critically wounded head and neck were every bit as repulsive as they were intimidating. With only feet between them, the decomposing tissue along her face, mouth, and hands put off a stench he had yet to experience. She smelled like death had come for her three days ago and she looked even worse.

"What the hell are you?"

He didn't think. He didn't pause and he didn't speak. Griffin reached into the mound of bodies separating him from the women and pulled. He pulled from the bottom and struggled against the weight and as they began to fall around him, the larger woman slid back and to the right, the flames at her back now completely enraged.

Laying on his stomach across three dead prison

guards, Griffin extended his arms and reached for Cora's hands. Still on her back, she clutched his wrists and began kicking at her attacker who'd righted herself and grabbed for her ankles yet again.

"Keep kicking," Griffin said as the larger woman continued to pull her way back toward them.

Still on her back, Cora kicked as Griffin pulled. The larger woman continued to claw at Cora's pant leg as Griffin braced himself and wound the orange jumpsuit around his wrists. "Look at me, and don't look anywhere else. We're getting out of here, right now."

Cora leaned back and through her upside-down view, locked eyes with Griffin. She didn't say a word as her thoughts were still with the woman tearing at her legs. Freeing her right foot, she was able to kick down and land a glancing blow against the right side of her friend's already disfigured face.

Coming back quickly, the incensed woman led once again with her snapping jaw as Cora landed another strike and then another. With her left leg trailing, the woman grabbed Cora's exposed ankle and began forcing it toward her mouth. As Cora again kicked out with her free leg, the woman bit down and came away with nothing but air.

Finding a foothold along the uneven surface he stood on, and with Cora nearly free, Griffin released his left hand and grabbed the railing near the bus's door. Anchoring himself, he quickly squatted down and tightened his grip on the orange jumpsuit. "Hold on."

Her calves cramped and her lower back began to spasm as Griffin pulled her away from her attacker. Up and over three more battered bodies and then crashing out into the open area at the front of the bus, the pair fell into one another. Griffin pushed back into the driver's area, knelt down, and helped Cora up and onto her feet.

Back to Cora's attacker, the mound of bodies shifted awkwardly, sending her to the bottom and burying her beneath four others. With only her arms and face now visible, Trish fought unsuccessfully to free herself from the crushing weight and the flames that finally consumed her. "She's gone," Griffin said.

Reaching out and taking his hand into hers, Cora said, "Thank you."

The bus lunged forward again as Griffin pointed toward the smashed out front windshield and said, "We gotta go, but watch your step."

Leading the way as they stepped through the jagged path toward the opening, Griffin looked over at the driver. Moving past the elderly gentleman for the second time, he would have sworn under oath that the dead man moved his eyes to follow them.

Stepping out first, he helped Cora to the opposite side of the road and sat her on the ice chest that had been ejected from the SUV. He leaned in, removed a four inch folding knife from his back pocket and cut the orange jumpsuit away from her wrists. "Okay, that's done."

Cora looked up and saw that he was smiling. Her only thought was that this man must be exceptionally happy to be alive. Any other explanation for his apparent joy when surrounded by all this death would be highly inappropriate.

Attempting to return the awkward gesture, she half-smiled, but quickly turned away and moved her line of sight to the shiny hardware binding her wrists to one another. "I really don't—"

Griffin placed his hand under her chin, lifted her head, and said, "I don't want to know and we really don't have the time. All that matters right now is that you and I are alive, but if we don't get down off this mountain and out of the snow, we won't be."

Cora nodded in agreement and started to stand.

Griffin moved his hand to her shoulder and shook his head. "Just rest for a few minutes and catch your breath. We've got a pretty good walk ahead of us and you're gonna need every last bit of strength you have. I'm not gonna let you slow us down."

Cora leaned against the tree at her back and attempted to brush the flaking blood from her hands. "Okay."

Griffin turned and disappeared back in through the front of the bus. He reappeared twice, again dragging a body with each pass. As the smoke continued to grow, he exited one last time, now pulling out one of the guards.

Coughing as he spat a mouthful of soot out onto the pavement, Griffin seized the guard's nine millimeter and her keys. Returning to Cora, he stared into her eyes and with his left hand, pulled a forty-five caliber pistol from his waistband.

Holding one weapon in each hand, he said, "I'm going to trust you here. I have no reason to, although I also have no reason not to. I don't know what the hell is going on this morning, and I really don't care, but I'm not taking any chances. However, if you even think about doing anything other than protecting yourself with this, I *WILL* end your life. Are we clear?"

She nodded.

"Okay then," Griffin said, holding out both weapons. "You have a preference?"

She motioned toward the forty-five and then looked back at her cuffs.

Setting the weapon at her feet, Griffin took the guard's keys from his pocket and knelt at her side. "Just so we're clear—"

"You can relax," Cora said. "That's not me."

Griffin released her cuffs and then handed them back to her. "Time to prove it."

She stood, hurled them across the road, and stepped to him. She raised her arms slowly and moved in close, their torsos making contact first. She laid her head on his chest and draped her arms around him. "My name is Cora and you are the first man I have touched in months. Thank you for saving my life, but you smell like two-day-old crap."

He instinct was to push her away, but he let the moment play out a bit longer. As she lifted her head and stepped back he said, "I'm Griffin. I think we're gonna get along just fine. Oh, and by the way, you're welcome."

14

Moving to the rear stairwell, Ethan grabbed the clipboard from the stainless steel hook, logged their departure time, and handed it to David before opening the door. They stomped heavily down the galvanized diamond-plated steps and into the rear lot. Still in possession of the keys, Ethan said, "I'm driving today."

"Oh boy," David said. "This thing with Shannon really has you wound up."

"Wrong, I just want to get this run done today and get back home; traffic is going to be a nightmare through downtown after lunch."

"Whatever you say buddy, but are you planning on making any stops before we head out of town?"

Ethan didn't answer as the pair stopped in front of the white armored truck they would use for today's run, and turned to face one another. Months earlier, David started a morning ritual that continued on to this very day. He and Ethan would remind each other of the seriousness involved with what they did every time they left the yard.

Even though most days they had little more than

a passing conversation with anyone other than the people they worked with, they knew that the cargo they were transporting had the potential to make each day on earth their last.

David raised his arms and slammed them into Ethan's vest. "Here we go my man. You and I. Out and back, in under five hours. Let's do this."

A smirk slid across Ethan's face as he in turn pounded his fists against David's body armor. "Together first, and together to the end. Let's do this."

As the men turned to walk to their respective sides of the truck, Ethan paused and added something of his own. Turning and shoving David from behind, he said, "And don't screw this up."

Laughing, David moved to the passenger side, slid his phone from his rear pocket, and climbed in. As Ethan fired up the steel plated behemoth, David powered on his phone. Looking out toward the western skyline and below that, the path they'd be taking out of the city, he said, "Starting to snow."

"Add that to the drive and I think you may just be right—my sister is definitely going to fire us today. Unless, that is, you allow me to drive the way I need to—"

Staring down at his phone, David interrupted. "Carly's texted me ten times in the last five minutes."

"I take it you did something stupid last night and now she's finally come to her senses, probably just realized she's way too good for you."

"Not exactly. She's at work and said she's scared.

That was her last text. She said they are getting overrun this morning and is freaking out about all the news coming in from the city."

Pulling out from the lot, Ethan stopped in the alley and waited as the massive gate closed. Looking over as David finished his reply and hit send, he said, "So, what'd you tell her?"

Still peering down at the screen, David said, "I told her we'd get back early and after we leave the bank, we'd stop by."

"We?"

"Just drive."

Down the alley and out onto Second, Ethan nodded toward the end of the block and the gathering crowd. "Can't wait till they leave tomorrow. I still don't know why this town has to host that cook-off every year. We lose more money than we make. I just pray that this is the last year."

"You say that every year."

"That's cause it's true. You don't even like it and you like everything and everybody."

"That's not true," David said. "But I do like going down there in the afternoon. Carly and I are heading over tonight."

"Yeah, sure you are. What'd you forget about the little gift you received after eating some out-of-towner's spoiled chili meat last year?"

"That was a stomach bug."

Turning left onto Main and then a second left on Third, they headed for the city limits. "No," Ethan said, "that was projectile vomiting, and if you'd like to steer clear of it this year, you may want to just avoid that mess altogether."

Even though this was the less direct route, and it would add an additional five miles, they'd still arrive at the warehouse in under ninety minutes. This would give the men an hour or two for loading and paperwork, two hours for the return trip down the mountain, and another hour to unload at the bank before driving back to the office. Ethan was confident they'd once again avoid his sister's wrath.

In the ten minutes since leaving the yard, they'd yet to run across another vehicle. Waiting at the final traffic signal before crossing over the city limits, Ethan motioned toward the town's oldest watering hole and its parking lot, known to every resident as Frankenstein's playground.

Years earlier after watching one unfortunate soul after another stumble around the parking lot outside The Red Moose Tavern, attempting to locate their vehicle, Sheriff Harris put together a video as a public service announcement and played it at the monthly town hall meetings.

The residents who were lucky enough to avoid being caught on video dubbed the others as Frankenstein's drunk relatives due to the way the fought to stay upright. The name caught on and spurred a new Friday evening ritual.

If one found themselves without much to do at the end of a long week, they could always join the half dozen or so others across the street from the Red Moose and take bets on who'd make it to their vehicle and who'd have to be driven home by the Sheriff. Some nights this was the most excitement one could have for miles.

This morning, two men were just beyond the first row of parking stalls, with one hovering over the other. The two appeared to either be wresting or locked up in some sort of misguided attempt at performing forced CPR. David sent off another quick text before looking up. "Is that Alfred?"

"No, it looks like Billy and Lamar. I guess they still haven't sobered up."

"Why are they still out here?" David said, turning back to his phone. "This couldn't be a carry-over from last night, there's no way. I saw them leaving long before we did."

As Ethan continued to watch, the man who Ethan had correctly identified as Billy Ralston sat up. His entire right arm, from fingertip to shoulder, dripped with blood. And turning toward the sound of their massive vehicle, he also had a face full of the same.

"Hey buddy."

Not looking up, David said, "Yeah?"

"Whatever it was that you saw this morning in the city—"

"Uh huh."

"I think it may have found its way here."

15

His breath froze as it left his mouth. It then floated away in miniature crystals and fought to pass through the deluge falling from the sky. The air was cold as it bit at the exposed skin on his face and arms. With each passing minute, the temperature continued to drop and although the jacket he'd given her was more than double her size, he knew she'd be needing it much more than he ever would.

Standing behind the bus as it continued to be pulled toward the steep slope at the edge of the road, Griffin again looked back at Cora. She sat in the shadows of the massive tree line at the opposite side of the road as quarter sized flakes floated down and kissed the top of her head. He watched as she rubbed her hands together, blew into them, and then repeated the process again and again.

The last several hours had blown by in the blink of an eye, even as the last five minutes seemed to play out in slow motion. Studying the landscape as the bus teetered at the edge of the forest, Griffin counted aloud. "Six... seven... eight. Wait no, there's another two or three over there." They needed to move and it had to be now.

Hurrying back across the street as Cora stood and dusted herself off, Griffin said, "Who was sitting at the back of the bus?"

"What?"

"It looks like ten, maybe fifteen people got out after the crash. You can see their tracks heading down that hill. I'm not sure what those other markings are, possibly someone with a broken leg. Looks like they were dragging themselves through the snow."

"It was women, just other women."

"Yeah, okay. But what I'm asking, I mean, do we need to watch for these other women? If we come across them. Do we need to be ready to defend—"

Interrupting, Cora said, "No, they weren't like that. If they got out and didn't stay around to help, they'll probably do anything they can to avoid us."

"You sure?"

"No, but I think we're gonna have bigger problems just getting off this mountain."

"How many of you on the bus?"

"Thirty-five—exactly thirty-five. Four guards, twenty-five inmates and six of those men that were dressed in the yellow biohazard suits."

"Biohazard suits? Why would they be transporting—"

"I don't know who they were or why they were at our facility, but they all evacuated with the rest of us. I think this was the third or fourth bus out."

"Evacuating? Why were they evacuating?"

"I'm not really sure. We had some women come in and I think they were sick; it spread really quickly. They said more and more people were showing symptoms. They didn't know what else to do."

"Seems like a bit of an overreaction," Griffin said. "For only a few sick people."

"They didn't tell us very much, I just followed the others and got on the bus." Looking back up the road and then at the bus that again pitched forward, Cora nodded toward the trees. "Shouldn't we get going? It's coming down pretty hard."

Griffin stared into her eyes, paused for a moment, and then looked down to the discarded cuffs at the edge of the road. "Staying along the highway is gonna take too long. We need to go straight through. If we don't stop, I'll bet we can make it to that town within a few hours."

Cora didn't respond. She only nodded and continued rubbing her hands together.

"Listen," Griffin said. "I don't know you and you don't know me. Once we get into that town, we can go our separate ways and you can be whoever you want to be. But let's just get there first."

"What about you?"

"The first thing I'm doing when we get down there is find a coffee shop."

"That's not what I meant." Cora looked down at the jacket he'd given her. "I can't take this and watch you freeze to death. Because, if you think you'll make it all that way with what you're wearing, you're—"

Holding up his index finger, Griffin smiled. "Give

me a second." He turned and strode off across the lightly dusted road. Just as he rounded the front of the bus and disappeared inside, it lunged forward and down, taking the SUV with it.

As the rear end of the bus moved by her, Cora felt the heat generated by the dying flames on her face and hands. She turned and ran toward where both vehicles left the side of the road, slowing as she reached the edge. "Griffin?"

The bus stayed connected to the SUV as the two slid down the short slope and quickly into a massive boulder just before the edge of the forest. What few windows were left intact from the initial collision, exploded on impact, sending tiny slivers of glass out into the air that were indistinguishable from the shards of snow falling to earth.

As her view of the area came clear, she focused on the front end. From where she stood, it appeared that the bus had pulled the SUV in and closed off the hole Griffin had entered multiple times.

Cora stepped quickly through the trail of shrapnel left behind, and called for him once more. "Griffin?" She turned the corner near the front and confirmed her suspicions. Both the drivers and passenger doors were torn off and the front end of the SUV had plugged the hole in the front of the bus. "Damn it."

Attempting to see over the top of the smaller vehicle and into the bus, Cora leaned on the hood and pushed herself up. Nothing—no Griffin and no movement of any kind. The massive grave was dark, save for the few spot fires toward the back. There was also no sign of Trish.

Sliding back down and moving around the opposite side of the SUV, Cora tripped as she stepped on a rock that slid out from under her. She ended up on her backside, both arms covered to the wrist in upturned earth and wet snow.

Pushing back to her knees, his throttled voice found her before she turned to see the two bodies fighting to get to Griffin. He had them at arm's length with the larger man's knee in his throat. His mouth moved, but no sound pushed through.

Only having seen him for a few brief moments as she boarded the bus and then again on her way out, Cora thought her eyes were playing tricks on her. The bus driver was dead. How he was battling with a slightly younger, albeit much larger man, wasn't just curious, it was impossible.

"Griffin, are you alright?"

Both men turned their attention away from Griffin and faced her. Their eyes glassed over in a shade not all that different than the snow plastered in patches along their blood-soaked faces. The bus driver pushed off Griffin's legs and limped toward her as the other also started to stand.

Furrowing her brow, Cora looked back at Griffin as he found his voice. She began to speak, but not before he cut her off.

"Cora... RUN!"

16

The signal at Third Street had cycled through two greens before Ethan turned away from the scene playing out in the parking lot of the Red Moose. His left arm slung over the door handle, and nudging David with the other, he said, "Billy Ralston, what do we do about him?"

Since noticing their vehicle sitting alone in the street, the man covered in blood had turned back to his victim. He clawed furiously at the motionless body below and came away with handful after handful of shredded flesh. Impulsively, he continued shoveling his reward quickly into his mouth, only pausing briefly to turn and survey the area.

Again, Ethan turned to his friend. "DAVID, LET'S GO. THIS IS SERIOUS."

His head buried in his phone, David scrolled through one message in particular as he continued to get notifications every few seconds. He read through while only briefly looking back at the parking lot and up to Ethan. "Yeah, I know."

"Okay," Ethan said. "What's the plan?"

His thumbs rattling off a response to the multiple

texts he was receiving, David spoke but did not look up. "Not sure just yet. Whatever is happening with Ralston is nothing compared to what's going on back in town."

"Where?"

Glancing away from his phone for a moment, David looked out the passenger window and into the side mirror, before quickly returning to his texts. "According to Carly it's going on everywhere."

"What... what do you mean? We haven't seen anything, or for that matter anyone, in the last five minutes?"

"Check your mirrors."

Dense black smoke sat somewhere in the distance. Below that, pulsing flames that stretched for what looked like two city blocks. "Looks like Saul's place or maybe out as far as Travers field."

"No, Carly says it's Saint Mark's. She's hearing that there are people inside and she can't get ahold of anyone at the firehouse. I guess the landlines keep going in and out. The boys are either already there or on another call."

Shaking his head, Ethan said, "This doesn't make any sense. How is this thing spreading so fast? This is the first we've heard about any of this."

David smiled. "That's true, but when was the last time you watched the news, or actually read a newspaper?"

With his attention pulled back out into the street, Ethan didn't respond.

"Ethan, I think we need to maybe put off today's

run—"

His focus shifting between the street, the parking lot, and his mirrors, Ethan removed his seatbelt and sat forward, resting his forearms on the steering wheel. He looked past David, out the opposite window, and then again back into the street. "Hey, uh... where'd Ralston go?"

David fired off another text and looked up. Nodding toward the parking lot across the street, he said, "Better question, where's Lamar?"

Both men were now gone. The only thing remaining from the vicious attack was a speckled trail of bloody mucus, which led out into the street and disappeared behind the vacant building nearest the driver's side.

Setting his phone aside as it again beckoned for his attention, David also removed his seatbelt and sat forward as Ethan pulled slowly out into the intersection. "This can't be happening; nothing about this make sense. Even Carly is scared and you know nothing freaks her out."

Both men craning their heads to the left, Ethan pulled even with the edge of the abandoned building and stopped. They spotted a red trail that ran up onto the sidewalk and disappeared into the recessed frontage of what was once a vintage clothing shop.

"They're gone, and I really don't see the point in trying to find—"

David shook his head. "No, we're not making this run today. I'll take full responsibility. I can't tell you what all of this is or what it means, but I do know the people of this town are going to need us here today. We have to do what we can to make sure that everyone is safe from whatever this is."

"Do we? Do we really have an obligation to the same people that—"

"Let's just allow the past to stay in the past, at least for today. Let's make sure everyone is safe and then tomorrow you can go back to feeling however you want about the residents of Summer Mill. But I'll bet you may just have a change of heart."

"You sure you want to deal with my sister? You gonna be the one to call her later?"

"Emma loves me," David said. "I'll bet she even gives me a raise."

"A raise? I thought you knew my sister?"

"If she finds out I actually convinced you to do something to help someone other than yourself, she may just nominate me for a Nobel Prize, and I may just win."

"I swear, I don't know why I put up with your crap."

"Because," David said, "who else you gonna find to drag your sorry ass to work every day and then help you find your way home every night. You need me more than you need that weapon on your hip."

Still looking out the window to the left, although unable to find where the two disappeared into the building, Ethan removed his foot from the brake. "Okay, I'll let you take the fall for this. And you're buying the first round later—"

A flash of red and then they were rocketed

sideways, Ethan slamming headfirst into the roof and then falling violently back into his seat. David was forced against the door at his right, and as the armored truck moved up onto two wheels, he bit down hard into the meaty part of his tongue.

The jarring impact tore free the passenger side quarter-panel on the armored truck as the massive vehicle they'd collided with came into view. Engine two, one of only three emergency vehicles to service Summer Mill, rolled to a stop not more than thirty feet away.

Ethan cut the engine and paused as Engineer Stratton opened the driver's door and stepped out into the street. He and David also exited their truck and began to make their way over to the damaged fire engine.

Ethan was familiar with every single man who wore a Summer Mill Fire Department uniform and his least favorite was the man he'd just cut off. Engineer Thomas Stratton, or Tommy to most anyone else, walked faster toward Ethan and David with each step. He swung his arms and pointed as the men drew near.

"Ethan Runner, I should take your head off. You have to be the dumbest—"

From out of the shadows afforded by the former antique shop came the men who'd disappeared moments earlier. The first and smaller of the two, tackled Tommy Stratton without warning and shoved him back-first onto the asphalt.

As Tommy struggled to get free, the second and

much more massive of the two men came in on top. Tommy's arms became a blur, moving side to side as he attempted to stave off their advances. He called out for help as the captain and firefighter moved in quickly on both sides, each grasping for one of the two attackers.

David started into a dead sprint heading toward the chaos as Ethan came in from behind. They both arrived as the men in blue fought to free their colleague from the bottom of the pile. The eldest of the city employees, Captain Faust, pulled at the larger of the two attackers. And upon losing his grip, the father of five stumbled backward and tripped over the curb.

Sliding into his spot, David reached out for the same attacker, although he was jerked from behind by Ethan. And as the two crazed men continued their assault, he turned to Ethan and threw up his hands. "What the hell are you doing?"

Pointing at the attack taking place three feet from where they stood, Ethan said, "What are YOU doing? Are you trying to get yourself killed?"

"Ethan, damn it, we need to help."

"It's too late," Ethan said, pointing toward the pile of bloodied bodies. "Tommy's gone."

Stepping to the right, David turned away as the smaller of the two attackers pressed his hand into his victim's eye sockets and pulled free a majority of his face and nose. Tossing aside his trophy, the crazed individual lunged forward and took a massive bite out of Tommy's throat.

Frozen in place, David hadn't noticed that the firefighter had also moved away and circled in from behind. He was caught off guard as the younger man grabbed his weapon from his hip and pushed him to the side.

The firefighter stepped to the two men taking apart his friend, raised the weapon, and put one round into the back of each of their heads. He then walked calmly back to David, turned the weapon on its side, and handed it back. "They don't die—they just keep coming and they kill everything in their path, unless you take out the head."

17

Irritated now more than worried, Emma sat at the kitchen table and visualized what she could not see. The streets leading home were much less of a monumental catastrophe than she remembered from the plane. A few minor collisions near the airport and more foot traffic than usual were the only things to catch her eye. Although for over half the trip, she had stayed glued to her phone.

The two men who delivered her to the front door and were now stationed inside the black Cadillac Escalade in front of her home hadn't spoken a word to one another or her for the entire twenty-five-minute trip. And that was just fine with her. She responded to each of Goodwin's messages and before reaching her neighborhood, tried again to contact her brother. Two unanswered calls to his cell, and one to the remote office in Summer Mill, had her massaging her temples as they turned onto her street.

Pulling to a stop along the curb, less than thirty feet from her front door, the driver remained with the SUV as the passenger exited with Emma. Gun in hand, he carried the larger of her two bags and stayed within five paces, glancing left and right as if they were already under attack. He waited for her to open the door, entered first, and made a quick sweep through the interior.

Going back out the way he came, the neatly dressed thirty-something gentleman nodded as he moved back past her and spoke for the first and only time. "Mr. Goodwin will send you my number, text if you need something, and no matter what, do not leave your home or unlock your door for anyone but me."

Not waiting for a response, he slid in through the passenger door and disappeared behind the blacked out windows.

.   .   .

Forty minutes had passed since walking through her front door, and her phone rang once again.

Unknown.

She glared at the screen and counted the rings. As Emma let the call go to voicemail, she looked away and caught the first few drops of rain as they dotted the bay window on the other side of the archway leading into the living room. Another sixty seconds and without the mystery caller leaving a message, she stood and walked back to her study.

Seated at her desk, she moved the mouse forward and woke the computer. As the screen came to life, the same error message taunted her for the fourth time since she arrived home. *Problem establishing secure connection, upload failed.*

Attempting to clear the message, she was unable to control her mouse as a dialogue box opened in the upper right corner of the monitor. *Emma, we've remoted to your machine. I cannot wait another minute for those files. We'll take it from here.*

"Goodwin."

Waiting for additional instruction, Emma began to type, although as she suspected he had control over her peripherals as well. Sliding the keyboard away and leaning back in her chair, an alert quickly pulled her back as the sound of another message rang through the external speakers. *"I've disabled your access for the moment. Once the data is retrieved, we'll get you back online. – MG"*

"Disabled my access, is he kidding?"

Back to the kitchen and her phone, Emma pulled up Marcus Goodwin's office number and with her right index finger, hovered above the call button. "There's a first time for everything. I guess if he gave me the number, he would expect that I may someday use it."

Changing her mind and setting the phone down, she walked into the living room, checked the time, and grabbed the television remote. Powering on, the first images to fill the forty-seven-inch screen caught her off guard. As of eight-fifteen, only three of the local news stations remained on the air.

The first channel she flipped by flashed images of soldiers attacking one another near the entrance to a military base. The area looked somewhat familiar, although with the amount of travel she'd logged over the last year, and the number of security checkpoints she'd run through, pinpointing the exact location would be impossible.

Settling on coverage of the events happening less than an hour away, her mouth dropped open as her mind tried to make sense of what was taking place at Sunny Acres. Along the greenbelt in front of the plush senior center, she witnessed a group of reporters tripping over one another as they attempted to pull away from a half dozen crazed senior citizens. As the over-seventy crowd pushed out into the parking area, they finally overtook the well-coiffed reporters.

The video feed skipped repeatedly just before the camera was dropped and three of the seniors fell onto the male reporter. As the group of four bodies skidded across the blacktop, it appeared as though the elderly residents were not just attacking the reporter, but actually trying to devour him.

The first disturbed senior lunged forward and bit into the reporter just below his jawline. And in pulling back, the woman with failing panty hose came away with what looked like a mouthful of the reporter's throat. As the station went to commercial, it appeared as though the others piling in from behind also had the same objective.

"What is this?"

Powering off the television, Emma tossed the remote back onto the couch and decided the call would be worth whatever penance Goodwin had in store. Through the archway and back into the kitchen, her phone rang before she even reached the table. Assuming it was the man who signed her checks, she was ready. "Okay, here we go."

Before depressing the answer button, she noticed the Unknown Caller again attempting to make contact. She quickly ignored the call and before losing her nerve, dialed Marcus Goodwin's office number.

The man who intimidated nearly every person he came into contact with answered on the first ring. "Yes Emma, why are you calling?"

Not completely prepared, she had dialed the phone out of frustration and anxiety. "Mr. Goodwin, I just wanted you to know that I tried multiple times to—"

"Listen Emma, I appreciate what you've done for this company, although with what's happening out there today, well... things are going to change."

The confusion in her voice was evident. "Is this something we did?"

Dead air.

Emma paused for a beat and asked again. "Mr. Goodwin, is what's happening out there related to Project Ares?"

She could hear his breathing on the opposite end and waited. He asked someone to close his office door and for the first time she had the sense that he was losing his calm. "What I've created is going to change the world. And with anything of this magnitude, there is always a price to pay. Some sacrifices will always be required—"

Interrupting, she said, "I don't understand, we weren't even scheduled to test for another month."

Again his tone intensified. "You need to realize that this project predates your tenure with this company by many years, and as such, you were only given the information required for you to do your job. Nothing more. What I would suggest is that you pull back on the accusatory line of questioning and settle in. The next few weeks could be very challenging."

"What are you saying, exactly?"

"I'm not the person most people think I am. This has proven to be an asset in business, although the perception of who I am is simply an illusion. There is no friend, no enemy, and no employer. I'm just a man who decided to make the world a better place, no matter what the cost."

Emma swallowed hard. "I'm not sure what—"

He was gone, the line dead before she had the chance to finish. Emma quickly redialed the number and after the ninth ring, the call disconnected. Glancing at the screen, her battery showed less than twenty percent. Setting the phone on the table, she moved back through the kitchen and into the study.

Seated in front of her monitor, she tapped the enter key and woke the computer. Again in control of her terminal, she was greeted with a new desktop background. Having been replaced by the stock background image shipped with the unit, the black and yellow logo of BXF Technologies was now simply a memory.

Without having to enter her username and password, she quickly navigated to the search window and typed in the name of the file she last worked on.

No results.

Back to the search function, she keyed in the name of the folder which contained her new hire documentation and the spreadsheets referencing her lab times for the prior ninety days.

No results.

Tossing the keyboard across the length of her desk, she stood. "Well, I guess that means no severance package."

Rubbing her temples and turning into the hall toward her bedroom, her cell phone rang for the third time in the last ten minutes. "Let me guess, Unknown Caller?"

18

The jacket sloshed from side to side as she moved between the trees. The ground covered in white powder seemed to be sliding under her in fast-forward as each step landed in the same distinct pattern, kicking up mud and snow as she carried on. Cora was running, but it felt more like she was simply falling forward, yet somehow still maintaining an upright position.

Passing yet another tree, she hadn't looked back to see her pursuers since turning and sprinting away. They were still there, that she knew. And they were close, close enough that their footsteps played like a bass drum against the inside of her ears.

Griffin had joined the chase as well, and as she fought her way around another small outcropping of something resembling miniature Christmas trees, Cora lost her footing. She slid sideways across a small section of ice that formed near the base of a large tree, and into a shrub the size of a small car.

With only her upper body exposed, and as the two repulsive men slowly progressed toward her, Cora rolled onto her stomach. Calculating the speed at which they limped forward and placing that against the time she needed to slide out from under the bush, stand, and get to the opening, the chances of her escaping the way she came in were zero.

Rounding the entrance to the small cove she'd slid into, the bus driver limped in first. His jaws were biting into the air as he pushed off the tree, rebounded back, and slowly stumbled toward the large shrub.

Pulling her knees up under her, Cora instinctively reached to her lower back and drew the weapon she'd been given. Steadying herself and quickly firing off two rounds, she blew apart the bus driver's right leg, just below the knee.

From somewhere beyond her field of vision, Griffin appeared like a silent freight train gliding through the night. Leaping the small overturned tree to her left, Griffin lowered his shoulder and collided into both men, the bus driver shooting forward and into Cora.

Pushed back into the underbrush, Cora fought to pull her arms free of the tangled mess the jacket had become in the broken branches. As she dug her heels into the loose earth, the bus driver lunged headfirst into the bush, but was caught twelve inches short of her chest. He again snapped at the air, as what looked like saliva, blood, and something a dirty shade of orange dripped from his mouth.

Her head on a swivel, Cora looked right and then left and back to the right as the madman above her began breaking through the branches, one small limb at a time. She'd dropped the forty-five as she fell backward into the bush, and although she was unable to locate it, she felt it was close.

Out past the bush, a grey streak rushed through from left to right, catching her attention. She watched as Griffin moved to his feet and fired off three shots into the abdomen of the second man giving them chase.

Stepping back and quickly turning his focus to the bus driver, Griffin hadn't noticed that the man he'd just shot began to push away from the ground.

"Griffin, look out."

Cutting his attention back to the left, he eyed the mortally wounded man with curiosity. And as the man he'd known for less than forty-eight hours stood and took two steps forward, Griffin raised his weapon. "Joe," he said, "I'm sorry."

Griffin placed the end of his weapon against the man's forehead and squeezed the trigger once. As the back of the man's head exploded into the white powdered backdrop, and before his body crumbled to the ground, Griffin turned and strode quickly to the bush.

Still entangled in the mess of broken twigs and with the arms of the oversized jacket holding her in limbo, Cora screamed. As the deranged man's face crept forward, she adjusted the tilt of her torso and with her arms locked, grabbed the sides of his shoulders, pressing upward.

Struggling to keep his mouth away from her folded collar, Cora again planted her left foot and used the unbalanced leverage to drive her right knee squarely into his man parts. Solid contact—the strike much more violent than she'd thought possible from her awkward position, vibrated from her hip all the way down to her toes.

Focusing on his milky white eyes as her leg drifted back down, the man above her didn't blink. He didn't flinch. He didn't even appear to acknowledge the contact.

Her hands now gripped tight to the thick material of the bus driver's jacket, she began to cramp. Sliding back yet again, she screamed as he lurched forward and buried his head in her right armpit. Through the three layers, she felt his lips fold back and his teeth grinding against the dense fabric.

Leaning back and facing Cora, the driver spit a mouthful of nylon and polyester into the wind, growling as he looked into her eyes.

The cold air now assaulting the exposed skin along her right side, Cora twisted to the left and searched for the man who'd saved her less than twenty minutes earlier. "GRIFFIN—"

"I'm here."

The driver, now with his hands around her waist, scratched at her belt and looped his fingers between the leather and the denim that sat next to her cool skin. The deep knurled ridges along his left hand oozed a warm river of blood that ran down her side and rested in the crevasse of her lower back.

Griffin's voice came from somewhere beyond. "Hold tight—I'll have you out in just a minute."

Only Cora didn't have a minute. She didn't have thirty seconds. From her position and with the incensed older man still bearing down, she was already out of time.

As the bus driver craned his neck forward and down, pushing into her bare right side, Cora slid both of her legs up under him, creating an ever so slight gap between the two. She wedged one knee up and then the other, until the space would accommodate the grimy soles of her tattered deck shoes.

She now sensed that Griffin had joined the absurd game of tug-of-war as the driver's body inched backward, placing his face directly over her open skin. "WAIT."

Griffin stopped pulling. "WHAT?"

Releasing her right hand from the driver's shoulder, Cora grabbed a handful of his hair and pushed his face to the left, and in the process ripped away a large chunk of his matted hair. Now free, his head again darted forward as she came around and drove her thumb into his left eye socket, pushing him back once again.

Undeterred, the driver pulled away and bit at her hand as his eye dangled a half inch out of its socket. Locking her toes under the waistband of the driver's trousers, Cora kicked up and away, sending him into the air, crashing into Griffin, and out onto the snow-covered dirt.

Cora scrambled out from under the tall shrub, retrieved the weapon she'd dropped, and stood over the man still frantically struggling to get at her.

Placing her foot over his throat as he clawed at her pant leg, she put two rounds into her attacker's head.

Dropping her weapon and sliding down the tree at her back, she turned to Griffin. "Why is this happening, what's wrong with these people?"

Griffin, who from his knees brushed off the filth of his own battle, said, "I don't know, but I have a funny feeling this isn't the end of it."

19

Helping carry the gravely wounded engineer to the rear door of the fire truck, no one spoke. Ethan and David only watched the captain and firefighter for signals on what they needed. They helped set the limp body in and slammed the door. The firefighter circled the rig as the captain moved to the driver's door. Before stepping inside, he turned to Ethan and David. "Boys, this thing is bad, I mean real bad. Get to your loved ones and find somewhere to hide, at least for a few days."

David nodded. "Where are you taking him?"

Shutting the driver's door and lowering the window, the captain said, "To the hospital, and after that the boys and I are going to take a wide run around town, just to make sure everyone who is able gets to somewhere safe."

"The hospital? But is he even going to make it—"

Starting the engine, the captain looked out to the horizon. "We've got to get out ahead of this thing. We've seen reports from other cities that this virus or whatever it is actually began yesterday, and some even the day before. Those places are no longer around. Their communications are dead and the streets are filled with people eating each other. That will be this place in a matter of hours. Get somewhere safe, and do it soon."

Ethan motioned toward the east end of town. "The firehouse, can't we all hole up there?"

Pulling away from the sidewalk, the captain shook his head. "It's already gone. Those things came through nearly an hour ago. Tore the damn garage doors right off their tracks. Once we make our last sweep, we're heading to higher ground, maybe drive into the city."

"But—"

"You boys should be fine. You have weapons—don't be afraid to use them."

David watched as the red behemoth moved out into the street and turned right a quarter mile up. He grabbed Ethan by the jacket, and looked him in the eyes. "Thank you."

"What?"

"For pulling me away, before I grabbed him. You're right."

"I am?"

David nodded. "Yeah, those things. I don't know. I mean. I mean you know, my head is still spinning, but, yeah. We have to listen to what Captain Faust said. We have to go get Carly right now and get the hell out of here. If we wait until tomorrow, it may be too late."

"We?"

"Yes we, what else are you going to do? You heard

him, we need to go."

Turning away from his friend and starting back toward their truck, Ethan said, "How do we know he's telling the truth about how widespread this is, or that any of what you saw online was the truth? We don't, all we have to go on is the word of a man who just lost one of his own."

Stepping up his pace, David moved ahead of his friend and stopped. "Listen, I'm going to get Carly, and you're coming along. I don't really care what you want and I'm not asking for permission. Get in the truck. Once we find a safe place to ride this out, you're free to do whatever you want. I'm your best friend and I'll be damned if I let this thing take either of us down."

Ethan sat quiet for a moment, looking at David but also looking through him. He rubbed his eyes and shook his head. "Okay, but there are two things we're doing before we leave."

"What's that?"

"We make sure Shannon is okay and go back to my apartment."

"For what?"

"I need to find out what Emma wanted last night. I'm now guessing it had nothing to do with work. I'll grab my phone and charge it as we drive."

Nodding, David held out his hand. "Sure thing, but this time I'm driving."

Ethan handed over the keys, moved to the passenger door and before stepping inside, checked his weapon. David did the same and made a mental note of the two additional magazines he left in the center console.

A hollow thud from the rear of the armored vehicle caused both men to step back. Yelling over the top of the truck Ethan pulled out his weapon and started to expand his radius around the back of the truck. "David, what the hell was that?"

Quickly opening the driver's door and climbing in, David turned over the engine before calling back to his friend. "I don't know, just get in. Let's go."

Ethan took two small steps toward the rear and stopped. Another jarring blow against their vehicle and another. He moved another few feet out and back as the offending party came into view. Six unmistakably devastated individuals, each more grotesquely malformed than the next.

The first three men had collectively, less than fifty percent of their faces still intact. From the chest down, they appeared somewhat normal, except for the bright red smattering that covered most of their shirts and pants. Any of the three could have been his next door neighbor, although today, Ethan wouldn't have been able to pick him out of a lineup.

Two smaller females were also part of the grisly collection, and appeared to have been gutted from sternum to navel. As they marched toward Ethan, what remained of their internal organs spilled out over their belts and dropped onto the street with each step forward.

The last member of the group, a heavyset gentleman, was most certainly an out-of-towner and was here specifically for the chili-fest. He wasn't nearly as disfigured as the others; his only distinguishing mark was the massive hole in his neck and the ensuing blood that flowed from his carotid. That and the '*Kiss the Cook*' apron offered Ethan a completely different reason to want to shoot him first.

Turning their attention away from the truck, the group eyed Ethan as he took another step forward and raised his weapon. "Back, all of you. Step back from the vehicle or I will shoot."

His door now shut and waiting for his friend to join him in the cab, David only heard Ethan's last four words. With the truck still running and in park, he shook his head, stepped out and moved around the front.

Spotting Ethan dead ahead and with the gang of six approaching from the rear of the truck, David's line of sight was blocked. He moved quickly around to the left in an attempt to get a better vantage, but was still left without an opening. "Ethan, shoot them."

Turning to David and then back to the group, Ethan fired off three rounds, although only two found their intended targets. The first took down the man in the apron, striking him just above the right knee and throwing him instantly to the ground.

The next round tore into the shoulder of the unidentifiable man just behind the first. A mess of tattered cotton and large chunks of flesh winged off the women behind him. Off balance, the wounded man tripped over his own feet and took two of the others with him in the process.

With the last two now only feet away, Ethan took a small step back and again leveled his pistol. Squeezing off a single shot, he flinched as the head of the bigger of the two men exploded, sending the body instantly to the asphalt.

As he calculated how the next few seconds would play out, Ethan cut his eyes to the left and looked for an opening. Time slowed as the last assailant, moving more quickly than he expected, lunged forward and slammed face-first into his chest.

His elbows made contact with the unforgiving roadway first, taking the full weight of both bodies and sending shockwaves up through Ethan's arms. His upper back touched down next, followed almost immediately by his head.

Sliding backward as the distressed individual clawed at his stomach, Ethan felt an all-too-familiar stitch. Originating deep within his right shoulder, it had been more than a decade since the last occurrence. Even though today's events forced an extra swell of adrenaline through every fragment of his six-foot, two-inch frame, he knew two things.

His shoulder joint had once again become separated, and there was nothing he could do with one hand that would keep the animal at his waist from ripping him apart.

20

She had questions, but at present there were things much more pressing than the exact details of how this all happened. Griffin grabbed the two lifeless men by the ankles and dragged them the short distance through the smooth snow, to the edge of the two-hundred foot descent.

Cora held both weapons and stayed at his side, watching their backs and scanning the slope above. "Why are you—"

"Hold on, let me do this first."

Checking the contour of the land below, Griffin charted the most likely route the bus driver's body would take as it plummeted down the steep ridge. Both flanks of the hillside seemed to funnel into one another, leaving only a few places where the bodies would come to rest at the completion of their unnatural journey.

Glancing back into the driving storm, Griffin paused and closed his eyes. "They're coming this way."

Tilting her head to the side and mimicking his movement, Cora said, "Who, who is coming?"

Sliding the bus driver's body to the edge, Griffin gave it a final shove and then watched as it began to cartwheel head over heels down the quiet snow-crusted embankment. "More like these guys. I'm guessing that your bus was carrying something other than guards and men in biohazard suits."

"Then let's go. Why are we wasting our time with this?"

Before sending Joe off to meet the bus driver, Griffin removed the man's jacket and slipped it over his damn near frost-bitten arms. "We are going. I'm just not going to make it easy for whoever is following us, you know, to actually follow us."

Cora looked down at the dried blood covering her hands. "Okay?"

Pushing the second body over the edge, Griffin watched as it covered nearly the same path as the first, but gained speed much more rapidly due to the extreme size difference. "Wow."

Looking back once more, Cora squinted. Attempting to focus through the falling snow and between the densely spaced spruces, she waited as her eyes adjusted to the varying highs and lows. "I don't get it, how do you know that anyone is even following—"

"They're here." Griffin said, moving away from the edge. "We have to go."

Stepping quickly to Cora, he placed his hands on her shoulders and squatted behind a large spruce. "We've got maybe a twenty second lead on them, but they know that we're here."

Eyeing his weapon and then her own, Cora said, "We have the advantage, why are *we* running from *them*?"

Griffin turned toward the now undeniable footfalls, coming from just beyond the treeline. "Because, I'm freezing. Because we have to get off this mountain in the next hour. But mostly because I still have no idea what the hell is going on, and whoever or whatever is following us doesn't seem to care."

Two silhouetted figures appeared not more than thirty yards away. They hadn't yet spotted the pair as Griffin pulled Cora into him. He spoke quietly into her ear and pointed to the open range to their right. "That's our only way down. You ready?"

"I don't know if—"

"There isn't time. I'd rather lose them than confront them. We can stop and talk about this once we're far enough away." Still standing in the shadows afforded them by the large spruce, Griffin stood and pulled Cora up by the jacket. "Let's go."

She followed him as the number of those in close pursuit increased to four and by the time they reached the open space, six. Although they moved at a slightly reduced tempo, the deep base of white powder blurred the advantage as Griffin struggled to keep up with his more agile counterpart.

Aided by the gradual slope, Cora ran out ahead. She focused on her breathing and tried to forget what this race meant. She wanted to block out the bus and what happened to her friend. She wanted to go back, to just wake up and have it all be a bad dream. She was running from something she didn't understand, but knew she needed to.

Breaking out from the trees and in full view, Griffin motioned toward the southern edge. "That's where we need to get to. It drops off over there and I don't think they'll be able to follow."

Nodding, Cora cursed into the falling snow. Her feet were two frozen slabs of concrete she wrestled to pull in and out of the snow. Not completely numb, the searing pain of a hundred thousand needles was running a close second to the inferno that now raged through both of her thighs. Each and every step tested her desire to continue forward.

Forty yards from the next grouping of trees and the air in her lungs began to thin. Her racing heart begged for mercy and the stitch in her side forced Cora to momentarily slow her pace. Turning to see the four disheveled women and two men closing the distance, she called to Griffin. "Where?"

Now alongside and matching her speed, he pointed with the nine millimeter still in his right hand. "The two trees right in the middle, get there first and I'll be right behind."

Reaching the rutted landscape near the outer rim of the open expanse, Cora pushed to stay ahead. She stepped lightly across the iced-over rocky terrain shadowed by the massive row of spruce. Consciously placing each stride in line with the one before and keeping her weight evenly distributed, Cora focused on the gap between the two trees. "Be careful, the ice."

Coming in less than a second behind Cora, Griffin only understood her warning as he began to slide. His right foot glided out from under him as he reached for the tree to his left. And crashing into her from behind, the disparity in their weight pushed Cora past the first row of trees and off the jagged ledge.

As she shot past the serrated edge of the hillside, the near vertical drop afforded her a brief moment to realize her new predicament. Large flat rock surrounded by loose shale and peppered with not nearly enough foliage to grant her a reprieve from injury, Cora clenched her teeth and braced for impact.

Her left foot contacted the ground first. Again propelled forward, Cora's knees slammed against the unforgiving rock face, sending her onto her stomach. Fighting to bring her arms up around her face, she skidded headfirst into a barren shrub the size of a small oven.

As she plowed through the dried out branches, her jacket took much of the initial damage. Flat on her back, shards of black nylon and puffed white feathers slowly floated back to earth as her pulse echoed against her inner ear.

"GRIFFIN." Collecting herself and waiting for him to answer, Cora rubbed her hands along her face and neck. Nothing noteworthy. Taking a deep breath in through her nose and attempting to roll onto her stomach, a searing blowtorch exploded from the tender skin just above her hip.

Instinctively grabbing at the half-inch thick branch penetrating her left side, Cora gagged. Drawing back her blood-soaked left hand, she took another deep breath and nearly lost consciousness. Lifting her head, she could see that the opposite end of the limb was still securely attached to the desolate shrub that enveloped her.

Her heart rate beginning to climb yet again, and Cora cried out. They were only four words, yet nearly impossible to voice. "Griffin, I need help."

She waited, but there was still no response.

21

As the first few flakes of the day's snowfall kissed the exposed areas along his face and neck, Ethan attempted to sit forward. He flexed his right arm and made a fist, relieved to find that the extent of his injuries were encapsulated in only his shoulder. After three such injuries over the last twenty years, he'd be able to repair the damage on his own, if only he could get the beast clawing its way toward his throat to find another victim.

· · ·

Friday, October 6th, 1995. Seventeen minutes into the most important game of his epic high school football career, Ethan Runner found out that his seventeen-year-old body wasn't necessarily invincible.

Lying flat on his back in the middle of the street, he flashed to the first time he suffered pain of this magnitude. The fourth quarter of what would be his final high school football game, a night that should have brought about no less than eleven full-ride athletic scholarship offers, became the crutch he'd carry for the next two decades.

From the huddle, he nodded as his best friend signaled the next play. Before turning back to the rest of his offensive squad, Ethan looked toward the four seats occupied by his parents, his sister Emma, and the woman who'd become his wife only a handful of years later.

Emma, his mother, and his girlfriend seemed to be buried in whatever gossip they felt needed their attention at the moment. However, as was always the case, his father leaned into the railing and made eye contact with Ethan. He smiled and looked toward the end zone. Ethan smiled and nodded before dropping his head back into the huddle and calling out the play.

"We're going big. Let's show these children on the other side of line of scrimmage why they should have never stepped off that bus."

His offensive line began to slap at their hip pads as he called the play. "Eighty-three blue goose, deep pocket, blast left, on two."

As they moved into position, Ethan again scanned the crowd. This time he looked toward the upper right corner, attempting to count the number of college scouts spaced intermittently throughout the local families enjoying their Friday night ritual.

They weren't hard to spot. Discreetly alone and most with a massive clipboard obscuring their faces, these individuals only took their eyes off the field when Ethan moved to the sidelines. Although he'd already made up his mind on which school he'd quarterback for the following season, his father told him to keep an open mind and visit as many schools as time would allow.

There were a total of six schools on his short-list. And even though many of his friends were staying local or heading to the West Coast, Ethan had his mind made up that he'd be tossing the pigskin for the Florida Gators. His trip to the Sunshine State over the summer sealed the deal.

As he settled in behind center and scanned the defense, the world around went silent as it always did. The other twenty-one players on the field were his to own. Ethan was told on more than a few occasions that his ability to read defenses, as the plays were actually happening, was unparalleled at his age.

Taking the ball and dropping back, he quickly accounted for the three closest defenders and pumped the ball, sending those most near back and onto their heels. Ethan then shuffled left and hesitated as his teammate sped up field, losing the last two opponents.

Six seconds ticked off the clock as Ethan took a step forward and stiff-armed the opposing number sixty-six, sending him face-first into the turf. Pausing for another second, he waited for the pocket to clear, dropped his shoulder, and shot forward through the small opening between his left tackle and guard.

Crossing the line of scrimmage, Ethan leapt one of the cornerbacks and turned up field. As he cut left and headed for the sideline, seven of the players on the opposing team were already too far behind to be of any real danger.

Less than a second later, as he was blowing by the fifty yard line, there was only one player left with any real chance of stopping him. Ethan's forty yard dash would be the best his school had seen in decades and only second to one other player in the entire valley. That player was now less than ten yards away. That player was the opposing number forty-two.

Cutting the field at a thirty degree angle, number forty-two was closer to the end zone, although Ethan was sure that one perfectly timed cut would put another six points on the scoreboard before the half ended. He only needed to stay on the gas.

At the twenty, the player now clearly making this personal, cut into his peripheral line of sight and moved quicker than anyone he'd played to date. As Ethan planted his left foot, just inches shy of the sideline, number forty-two left his feet, the red stripe along the top of his helmet in a direct path with Ethan's right arm.

Switching the ball to his left hand, pushing off, and raising his right arm, Ethan met his opponent at the six yard line. Attempting to force them both into the end zone, Ethan leaned into the collision, sending both he and his opponent airborne.

Number forty-two's helmet stuck Ethan just below his armpit and continued upward, forcing his elbow and forearm over his head. As they re-entered the atmosphere and were thrown into the grass, he slid headfirst to the three yard line, as fragments of sod and soil caked in around his facemask.

Twisting to the right and attempting to push himself up, Ethan only was able to pull free his left arm. As number forty-two scampered away to rejoin his team, and the crowd's applause began to die off, Ethan rolled to his back and sat forward.

This sensation was different. It was definitely a nine on the pain scale, maybe a ten. However, it was also infused with a dash of emptiness, almost as if his right shoulder was falling asleep. This was something he'd never experienced in this section of his body. Ethan attempted to place his hand on the ground to support pushing back to a standing positon, although his right arm refused.

His second effort placed him flat on his back, cradling his right arm in his left. And as the crowd went deadly quiet, the only voices were those of the overly exuberant crickets serenading one another, somewhere out in the late summer night.

Before the distant footsteps came bounding across the field toward him, Ethan regained the feeling along his left side. A rush of warmth was closely followed by a shock wave that raced from his shoulder into his neck, and exploded against the back of his skull.

His heart rate climbed with each second that passed and as he fought to take each new breath, a familiar voice broke the silence. "Hey buddy, I'm here."

His father was the first to reach him and kneeling

at his side, gently took Ethan's right hand. "Your shoulder?"

Two quick short breaths. "Yeah dad. It hurts real bad."

"I saw the hit son, it's probably separated. But hey, we'll get you to the hospital and fixed up before you know it. Just hang in there."

On the stretcher and escorted along the outer edge of the track, Ethan's breathing slowly began to return to normal. Hesitantly looking out over the crowd as the game continued, he watched as four of the six scouts packed their things and without making eye contact, hurried out of the stadium.

Wheeled into the emergency room with his father at his side, Ethan waited for the doctor and the nurse to vacate. As they slid the privacy curtain around his bed and the pain meds started to do their job, he had only one thing on his mind. "Dad?"

"Yeah?"

"The scout from Florida, did you talk to him? Is he still here?"

"Your mother has been trying to reach him at his hotel since the game ended."

Only half wanting to know, Ethan said, "Dad, do you think I'm done? I mean this is my throwing arm."

His dad smiled. "It won't be easy, but you will come back from this. The pain you're feeling is only temporary. Ethan, you were born to be a leader. So, when we leave this hospital, I want you to hold your head high and act like one. Show everyone in this valley who you are by doing what you need to do to get back on that field. Let your actions be your words."

.   .   .

The man clawing at his waist was now gone and as the rapid gunfire died off, David came into view, now standing over him. "Buddy, you nearly got yourself killed. How's your head?"

Back on his feet and moving slowly past the six corpses, Ethan said. "My head is fine, it's my shoulder, and it's out again."

"Well," David said, "then it's a good thing we're headed to the hospital."

As David helped him back into the passenger's side of the armored truck, Ethan thought back to that night twenty years before and only wished he'd have taken his father's advice.

22

Eyeing the edge of the cliff nearly thirty feet above, she waited for Griffin to appear; he didn't. Five minutes maybe ten, she wasn't sure, but it felt like time slowed to a crawl. She called out to him numerous times and after all she'd seen over the last ten years, it almost seemed absurd that she needed anyone's help. Least of all from a man.

Onto her right elbow, Cora torqued her shoulders left to get a glimpse of her predicament. Through the mess of blood and dirt clinging to her jacket, she could see where the branch pushed out of the ground, traveled eighteen inches, and then buried itself into her left side. The actual wound wasn't visible, however the rib-splitting agony confirmed that she had more to worry about than her lost partner.

Lying back down, Cora slid her right hand into the pocket-sized gash along the front of her jacket and pulled free several lengthy strips of the black nylon fabric. She tied them end to end and then retrieved two large handfuls of the inner lining from just above her waist.

As the initial shock began to wear off and the area along her left side flowed a steady river of blood, Cora closed her eyes. She focused on each individual breath and counted to ten. Checking the rock-face one last time, she spotted something that wasn't there two minutes before.

It was his arm. From the forearm down, it was Griffin. It wasn't moving and although normally that would be cause for alarm, she was relieved to see it motionless. It meant that those chasing them weren't hovering over his body tearing him apart. If they were, there'd surely be some sign. At least she hoped.

With the black nylon tied into a three-foot strap, Cora snapped off a pencil-sized branch that hung just above her head and placed it between her teeth. Setting the jacket's lining near the entry point along her left side, she slid the strap over her back, wiggled it behind her, and down to her waist.

"Now or never."

Sliding her legs back, Cora placed her feet against the twin mounds of granite at her left and bit down hard into the six-inch limb. Digging her heels in as tears rolled down her cheek, she reached overhead and anchored herself to the largest branch she could find.

As she pushed away, the sound of her anguish echoed through the valley below and then came rushing back just as fast. Pulling free of the limb impaled along her left side, Cora rolled onto her stomach and dropped her head to the ground.

Spitting out the small stick, Cora slowly backed out of the bush, wiped her face, and sat looking up at the steep hillside. Her pulse soared as she pulled her jacket up and fastened the length of nylon around her waist. Struggling to take a breath, she reached in and forced the jacket's lining into the space between her wound and the makeshift strap.

Light-headed and not quite ready for what came next, Cora winced as she leaned forward and used the short ledge to help her stand. Scanning the area to the right, she found a slightly less aggressive route back to the top. The slight angle meant not having to actually climb, giving her an opportunity to possibly repay her debt to Griffin.

Testing her strength, she stepped first with her right foot and waited for the flood of pain. To her surprise, only a slight twinge shot along her left side, and nothing more. Not wanting to under-compensate for the opposite side, she raised her left foot and matched the arc traveled in her first step. Twice the volume of pain as the first, but nothing to write home about.

Three more slow steps and then out into the soft underbrush at the right side of the cliff, Cora took another head-clearing breath before starting up the incline. So far, so good. The pain was tolerable and in lifting her jacket once again, she could see that the flow of red velvet along her left hip had slowed considerably.

She'd reach Griffin in a matter of minutes, and although she hadn't seen any movement from above, this was something she needed to do. One foot in front of the other, Cora moved in a zig-zag pattern through the awkwardly spaced trees, her left hand keeping pressure over the injury.

Not wanting to alert those in pursuit of her presence, but with the need to defuse her growing fears, Cora put a voice to her concerns. "Griffin."

She spoke quickly, while attempting to keep her voice from carrying. "Are you okay?"

Although she hadn't expected a response, she slowed and waited between two large spruces and listened to the passing storm move through the treetops. Nothing but her heart beating against the inside of her chest as Cora shook her head and started again.

Three feet from the crest and around the last tree, she spotted his boots. Another few feet beyond that, one of the women from the bus, clawing at the ground and inching toward him. Without another foothold in sight, Cora used both hands for leverage, and swung herself up and onto the open ledge.

The tenderness at her left side resurging, she clutched her hip and moved without caution to Griffin's side. Flat on his stomach, his arms and legs jutted out in four different directions, but looked to be injury free. She laid her hand on his back and exhaled as she felt the rise and fall with each new breath.

Pulling the hair away from his eyes, the bruise running from just above his right brow and ending at his hairline was beginning to swell. His lids fluttered as she leaned in and spoke quietly into his ear. "Griffin, wake up. I need to get you off this mountain, but I can't do it by myself."

Turning back to the woman now only inches from his legs, she was able to see where the others that followed had met their end. Putting the pieces together, it looked as if the ice-slicked rock formations were as much of an ally to Griffin as they were to his downfall.

Three of the six that gave chase were obviously eliminated by Griffin, as evidenced by the bloodied, grapefruit sized rock sitting at their feet. It appeared he must have used the slippery surface to take them to the ground one at a time, and then rapidly extinguish what remained inside.

With the last two nowhere to be found, Cora had a more pressing matter that needed her attention. The woman at their feet now had a hand hold on Griffin's pant leg and began to pull him toward her. Cora grimaced as she rolled Griffin onto his back and away from the disturbed woman.

Her left hand on her hip, she used the other to drag the flailing woman across the frozen granite, to where the earth dropped off. As the woman clawed furiously at the air, striking Cora's right pant leg repeatedly, she carefully slid her over the ledge. She paused a moment to watch the woman slide slowly into the same outcropping that had assaulted her minutes before.

Ten feet away, Griffin began to cough. As she hurried over, he arched forward and began to dry heave. Kneeling at his side, Cora held his hand and waited for the episode to pass. He didn't look good, but at the same time his eyes were now open, he was breathing, and for the moment was somewhat coherent. "Griffin, can you hear me?"

He nodded as he brought his hand up over the goose egg protruding from his forehead. "Yeah, I'm okay, what happened?"

"Too much to go into now. How do you feel?"

"Nauseous," he said. "And my head feels like it went through the garbage disposal."

"Can you walk?"

"I think so, but it doesn't really matter. We both have to get up right now."

"What?"

"There's more coming."

23

Belted into the passenger seat, Ethan held David's phone and read the rapid-fire texts that came through. "Carly's going to meet us near the nurse's station as soon as she can. But she said that you may have to help me pop this sucker back in, she's a bit buried at the moment."

"Wouldn't be the first time."

They'd be pulling into the parking lot in less than sixty seconds, but were warned to come through the employee entrance along the back of the hospital. The events happening at the main entrance left the already overworked hospital staff without any additional resources.

Entering the staff parking lot, David slowed to a stop and nodded out the left side of the truck. "Uh... Ethan."

Looking up from the phone as another text came through, Ethan understood why they'd stopped. "Keep going, we can't help them now."

Engine Two sat just shy of the next intersection, and less than one hundred feet from the main entrance to the hospital. Their rig had been, and was still being, attacked by more than two dozen out-of-towners. Men and women still wearing their chef's hats and chili-fest themed t-shirts forced their way into the cab.

The group of deranged individuals had pulled the firefighters out into the middle of the street and were huddled in tight packs over the two obscured bodies. Fighting one another for position, the frantic visitors clawed their way to the downed civil servants, shredded their dark blue uniforms, and began attacking the areas of exposed flesh.

"Feeders," David said. "It sure fits those things."

"What?"

"That's what they're calling them—Feeders."

"So that's what stayed with you from those videos, the pointless name that they came up with? Yeah, I get it, they feed on people, so they're Feeders. I'll call them whatever you want. But, what about the fact that those things seem to be multiplying faster than rabbits in spring? You need to move this truck before they decide to come feed on us."

"Ethan, we have to do something. We can't just leave them here to—"

"You gonna do it alone?" Ethan said. "Because I won't be any good to you out there."

"They were our friends, our neighbors. How are you okay with—"

Again interrupting, Ethan said, "There's what, thirty of them out there, maybe more? You really think we'd even have a chance? Listen, I'm getting my ass into that hospital, putting my shoulder back where it belongs, and getting the hell out of this city. You need to get Carly and do the same."

"I don't like it, but I guess you're right. I'm just not cool with leaving them out there."

"Those men—our friends—they're gone and there isn't anything we can do about it. Those other people, the ones attacking our friends were probably regular people too, but unless we want to end up like one of them, we need to think about us."

Shaking his head, David looked away and pulled to the rear of the lot. Away from the other vehicles he stopped, cut the engine, and checked his mirrors. "You ready?"

Ethan looked up from the display and handed David his phone. "Change of plans. Carly is locked in the administrator's office. She says it's too late, they've been overrun. She's hiding with someone named Ben. I texted her that we're on the way and to stay put."

"Okay," David said. "But, I'm still gonna to need your help, so..."

Unbuckling his seatbelt, Ethan reached for the door handle. "So what?"

"We've got to do your arm right now, before we get inside. You good with that?"

"Sure, but after this, you're going to help me. No questions asked. Are *you* good with that?"

Again checking the mirrors, David nodded and opened the door. "Let's do this." Looking back as he closed the door, he watched as Ethan also stepped out and headed toward the rear of the truck.

They met at the rear door as David checked his weapon, scanned the lot, and waited for Ethan to get in position. "Let's go bud."

Surveying his side of the lot, Ethan quickly holstered his weapon. He turned to David, rotated forward, and dropped his right shoulder. "We've got company. I'll get my shoulder back in, just get over here and cover me."

David stared at Ethan for a moment, offered a slight grin, and moved out around the passenger side of the vehicle. Turning back, he quietly said, "Maybe thirty seconds. We've got a pretty big group headed this way."

"I only need five." Arching his back and rounding his shoulder, Ethan clenched his jaw and breathed out forcefully through his nose. Beginning to externally rotate his right elbow, he closed his eyes and waited for the familiar jolt and the sound that could be heard three streets over.

"Ten seconds Ethan, it's now or never."

The pain nearly bringing him to his knees, Ethan yelped as his upper arm grinded through the last second of bone on bone before falling back into place. Spitting a small amount of blood out onto the pavement, he grabbed David, and pointed to the employee entrance. "Come on."

As sensation intermittently flowed in and out of his right arm, Ethan started toward the building with David close behind. They weaved their way through the abandoned vehicles littering the employee lot and upon reaching the rear entrance, pulled open the doors.

Securing the entrance, David retrieved a few sheets from the supply cart and tied off the double doors. Peering back out into the lot, many of those that followed had gotten disoriented as they made their way through the vehicles and had begun walking in circles, no closer to the building than they were sixty seconds before.

"Where'd Carly say they were?"

"One of the offices, I think up front. Let's find her and get the hell out of dodge."

Through the second set of double doors, and into the main hallway, David pulled out his phone. "Okay, I know where she is. Let's cut through the cafeteria and avoid the patient rooms altogether."

Tapping his friend on the shoulder and pointing toward the end of the lengthy corridor, Ethan placed his hand over his weapon. "What do you make of this?"

Two rows of aluminum-framed cots lined the darkened hall, one on each side. As close as he could estimate, there were thirty-six in total, each supporting a lifeless corpse and draped over in white hospital linen. And near the end of the unnerving gauntlet, David detected movement. "Carly, didn't mention any of this, but I have a feeling we're about to become educated, like right now."

24

The storm continued to grow. Pushing across the mountain in large flurries, it had nearly erased the foot shaped imprints left behind from their previous battle. Across the open glade, frosted treetops groaned under the burden of the snow resting innocently along its upper branches, releasing its overages back to earth with each new gust.

Their two yet unaccounted for pursuers had once again picked up the trail; however, they were now accompanied by three new friends. Punching out into the open, they now had a visual. Neither the terrain nor the inclement weather appeared to slow this new group.

Rubbing his head, Griffin leaned into Cora and stood. "Where's your gun?"

Without running her hand along her back to confirm her suspicions, she knew it wasn't there. Replaying in her head what she could of the previous thirty minutes, she figured it was either resting underneath the shrub she'd extricated herself from or buried beneath the new snow somewhere between here and there. "I don't know."

As the group of five again moved closer, Griffin turned back to the ledge. "We need to move, let's go."

"No," Cora said, grabbing a fistful of Griffin's jacket. "We won't make it down that way."

His head still in a fog, Griffin followed Cora as she cut a path through a dense row of mountain sagebrush. They stepped carefully away from the slick granite, finding their footing among the soft underbrush. Neither turned to check their progress, although as they advanced down the frozen hillside, using one another to stay upright, the distant footfalls grew closer.

Clutching the nine millimeter as if their being overrun was inevitable, Griffin motioned out of the next line of trees and to the left. With Cora's pace beginning to falter, they needed another plan. Outrunning those at their back wouldn't be an option for much longer. And for all they knew, this wasn't the only group hunting them.

Slowing, but continuing to ignore those in pursuit, he waited for Cora to come to him. Sliding up under her right arm, he spoke to her as they again were on the move. "We can't outrun them, and I'm not sure we'd do any better stopping to take them on with only one weapon."

Less composed than her counterpart, Cora fought to get the words out between heavy breaths. "What then?" Swallowing air in big gulps, she tried again. "What do we—?" The hole above her left hip now exacerbated by the contractions coursing through her abdominals, her voice broke with each word. "Then. What. Do. We. Do?"

Leaning into her, Griffin guided them through a dense patch of Rocky Mountain Juniper, hoping to make up ground through the speckled maze. His feet now completely numb, thoughts of frostbite and losing parts he was still fond of ran at the front of his mind. "We have to get out of this damn weather. Either that or hide, and I don't think—"

Her shoulders fell and as she breathed out into his ear, she stopped. Cora held tight to Griffin's shoulder as he urged her on. She said, "I can't feel my hands or my feet and if there was anything left in my stomach, I'd throw it up."

Griffin continued to drag her for another twenty feet before he also gave in. Out from under her arm, he turned and held her by the shoulders. "Can you stand?"

Tiny beads of sweat pooled at her hairline, then started down her forehead before evaporating into her thick black brows. Although now stationary, her breathing increased and as pale as the snow beyond, her face suddenly went flush. "I don't—" Her body dropped out from under his hands before he could grab ahold.

"CORA."

Nothing.

Down to his knees, her peered into her eyes and watched her irises fade into thin brown rings just before her lids dropped over them. "CORA, LET'S GO."

Again nothing.

Scanning the narrow margins between the white fluffed Junipers, Griffin slid her upper body onto his thighs. Her body convulsed as he felt his way to her carotid and applied enough pressure to confirm she was still present. "Okay, stay with me. We're getting out of here."

As the first of their five pursuers trudged out into the open, Griffin had already pulled her another twenty-five feet. At his back, a row of Ponderosa Pine large enough to hide a small plane rose out of the earth nearly thirty feet.

Plowing through the snow blanketed lower branches, he flinched as buckets of the white powder slipped in between his last layer of clothing and onto his bare back. Shielding Cora from much of the deluge, he looked back one last time before disappearing into the treeline. "You gotta be kidding me."

Two out in the open and both had seen them. He had five seconds, maybe ten to figure out what to do.

Propping her up against the base of the tree, Cora smiled. She was still here, at least for the moment. "Are we there?" she asked.

"Yes," he lied. "Just stay here and sleep. We're almost home."

Before heading back out into the unknown, Griffin quickly recounted the items left inside the jacket now draped over Cora's diminutive frame. He unzipped the right pocket, withdrew a black Patagonia wool-lined beanie and slipped it down over her head. She didn't react. Her eyes were still closed and with one last look at the rise and fall of her chest, Griffin pushed through the trees.

There were two, and then three. They moved slower than before, but came from opposing directions, essentially closing off any chance of exiting to the north. The first two, coming in from the left, were a few paces behind the leader as he made eye contact with each individually.

Pacing right, Griffin waited as they turned and started toward him. "Let's go, that's right just keep coming. I've got a surprise for each and every one of you."

Continuing to follow his every step, the group trailed him out away from Cora's shelter and into the next clearing. As Griffin quickened his pace and moved to the center, the leader growled. Baring her teeth, the former prison worker moved closer, exposing the jagged mess her teeth had become. Twisting her head curiously to the left, ragged pieces of flayed skin and an orange tinted mucus hung awkwardly from her mouth.

The group of three were now within a few feet of one another and less than a car length behind. His plan was to bring them out away from his traveling partner, use the open space to scatter the echoes from the three shots he planned to take, and then blow the backs of their heads into oblivion. In the off chance the other two were anywhere within earshot, they'd likely not find this location until he was back to Cora and off the mountain.

"Let's go ladies, just a few more feet."

Raising the Glock 17 nine millimeter pistol, Griffin sighted his first target. "Oh no."

On the outer edges of the glade, weaving in and out of the giant pine, were two more women from the bus. Dead eyes and branded in blood, they obviously hadn't come to help. They were also much closer to Cora than he was comfortable with.

"Here we go." Firing three close-range head shots, Griffin turned and ran as the trio of faceless, blood-saturated bodies dropped into the ankle-deep snow.

25

The sweet stinging stench of antiseptic crept into his nasal cavity, partially blotting what drifted from the three dozen corpses lining the rear hall. What did make its way through forced Ethan's hand up over his mouth and nose, gagging as he looked back at David. And finally nodding toward the end of the hall, he slowly lowered his hand. "The last cot on the right, looks like we're gonna have some company."

The blood-speckled white linen sheet shifted from side to side, as whatever it covered attempted to free itself. An arm dropped off the side of the cot and then both legs. The sheet folded into itself and then slipped into a heap next to the wall, as the man with less than half a face pushed away from the wall and attempted to right himself.

The overhead fluorescent lights flickered, illuminating the man who stood slightly above six and a half feet tall. Summer Mill's largest resident moved slowly into the center of the hall, turned toward Ethan and David, and sniffed at the air. The skin along his severely disfigured face hung in thick swatches and his eyes... had both been eaten out of their sockets.

Stepping into the recessed doorway to the right, Ethan motioned for his friend to follow. "Isn't that Franklin?"

.   .   .

They'd known the gargantuan beast, still clad in his shapeless denim overalls and shredded flannel long-sleeve shirt, for nearly their entire lives. The slender young man who initially strode into their first grade classroom carrying a lunch sac fashioned from a discarded pair of his older brother's trousers somehow grew into the biggest human Ethan or David had ever laid their eyes on.

As a youth, the son of a millet farmer came to be known by only his last name. Leslie Franklin had only ever answered to his given name once. In front of eighteen other snickering six and seven year olds, he corrected Mrs. Belzer. From the second morning he attended Summer Mill Elementary school, the boy with the abnormally long torso was just "Franklin".

As gentle as a mother hen, and without a callous cell in his body, the younger Franklin was nearly invisible to his peers. He stepped through adolescence without so much as raising his voice to his classmates or teachers. He blended in and never spoke first. He wasn't embarrassed by his given name, he just "liked Franklin better." And no one, including those who normally would, questioned it.

The giant man who'd never used his imposing size or strength in an aggressive manner stepped slowly through the draped cots. He continued forward with his nose in the air as heavy trails of black blood ran from the holes in his face. He bit at the air and growled as his right foot caught the leg of cot number twelve. Reaching down with one hand, the angered beast who was once the most reserved boy in town gripped the makeshift bed and tossed it, along with its occupant, nearly fifteen feet backwards and into the wall.

.   .   .

Leaning out of the shadows and into the hall for a second look, David said, "Yeah, that's Franklin alright, at least it used to be. Uh, and I think we're gonna need to find another way."

"What?"

Taking Ethan by the collar and holding his head out into the hall, David said, "You wanna try to get past him?"

Holding up his pistol, Ethan said, "He can't see us, he doesn't even know we're here. You could take him out from here. Put one into his head and then let's go get Carly."

As the behemoth stepped to within twenty feet, David stepped back into the alcove and gripped the door knob. "Of course, it's locked."

"David, just shoot him."

"No. We do that and every single one of those things knows exactly where we are. If it were just him, maybe. But we don't know what the rest of the building is like. Carly said she is hiding and I'm sure she's not doing it just to play games. We need to get to her without making ourselves another target."

"But—"

"And now that you bring it up, what's wrong with *your* weapon?"

"No, you're right," Ethan said. "We need to move through here without too much racket. So—"

"That's not what I meant and you know it. Back there in the street, you hesitated. You know what those things will do to you and to me if they get ahold of us."

"Yeah, but I—"

"That's not all," David said. "You also missed at least two shots."

"Yeah so, it happens."

"Not with you. You never miss. I've seen you uncap a bottle of Jack at fifty yards. You know that, so why now? What's with you?"

"I don't know," Ethan said. "I just can't seem to wrap my head around the fact that these people aren't actually *people*. They were living breathing humans less than a day ago, and now what, we're just supposed to kill them? Just put a bullet between their eyes and walk away?"

"If we're lucky." David leaned out once again and then looked at his watch. By his estimation, they had less than ten seconds to decide what they were going to do and how they were going to avoid their old school mate as Leslie Franklin staggered toward them. "Listen, I have no idea what's happened here and why people are acting the way they are, but as much as I hate saying it, we need to worry about us, and no one else. I would have thought that after the year you've had, it wouldn't be so hard to pull the trigger."

The words felt wrong even as they left his tongue. And as Ethan bit into his lip and shook his head, David reached out. Laying his hand on his friends shoulder, he spoke before Ethan could respond. "Buddy, I'm sorry. That was totally insensitive. I really shouldn't have—"

"It's okay. You're probably right. Let's go get Carly."

The thunderous footfalls out in the hall now quite obvious, David gently shook on the door handle and pressed his ear to the cold steel. Turning back to Ethan, he said, "Alright, we need to go. Whatever or whoever is on the other side of this door now knows we're out here. So I say we go with the known threat out in the hall. I'll take down the big guy and then we move through the rest of the building like we're on fire. You good?"

"What about not making any noise?"

David peered back into the hall and quickly pulled back. "I think it's too late for that, just promise me one thing."

Ethan readied his weapon. "What?"

"If I ever turn into one of those things, please take me out before I hurt anyone." And looking directly into his best friend's eyes, David said, "Promise me. I want you to say it."

Ethan faked a smile. "Yeah, okay. I promise to

shoot my best friend in the head if he tries to eat my face off."

As the overhead lights blinked again, the stench of their childhood friend rounded the corner only slightly before his darkened shadow blotted out what illumination remained. And as David stepped in front of Ethan, he raised his weapon and found a spot between the two gaping holes where Franklin's eyes should have been.

26

She didn't remember drifting off, however lying flat on her back, enveloped in the light-weight Siberian Down Comforter, it was easy to understand how it happened. With less than three hours of continuous sleep in the last day and a half, Emma just wanted to stay in bed.

She would have estimated it to be late afternoon, although up onto her right elbow and turning toward the clock, she'd only been away from her phone for just over two hours. The short unavoidable nap wasn't nearly long enough, but with the images from the news still fresh in her mind, and the possibility that BXF was somehow involved, she tossed her feet off the bed and stood.

Across the antique European Brushed Oak flooring, she strode into the bathroom, opened the spigot, and looked into the mirror as the water warmed. Staring into her own reflection always brought a sense of peace, centered her, and brought her back to her childhood. Having nearly identical facial features of her mother, she sometimes spoke into the mirror as if they were face to face.

"Mom, I pray that you and dad are alright. I don't know what's happening out there, and when I'll see you again, but I want you to know that I love you."

Patting the warm water against her face and neck, Emma reached for a hand towel, dried off, and before turning, stared at her own image once again. "For them, for all of them."

Into the hall and stopping at her study, she scanned the room. As it came to her, she moved to the filing cabinet and knelt beside the lower drawer. Sliding it open, movement beyond the trio of frosted twelve-inch square windows caught her eye. She focused on the last window as the light came through in fits and starts. "Must be the trees again. They should have cut them back by now."

Flipping through the individual files, she found what she was looking for. Precariously labeled "Research – Project Ares" she pulled out the inch-thick file and set it aside. Quickly rifling through what remained at the bottom of the drawer and then into her personal files, the second folder was nowhere to be found.

"Must have left that one at the office, damn it."

Stepping back into the hall, shadows again danced beyond the study windows as she started for the living room. Before heading into the kitchen, she turned on the television, hoping for a bit of background noise, but all that remained was a snowstorm of static. Every channel from local broadcasts through the bigger cable networks had gone dark.

Moving to the cordless phone near the front door, she pressed the talk button. Nothing. No dial tone. No incessant alarm that typically signals a low or dead battery. Just dead silence.

Placing the handset back in its cradle, Emma turned and moved back into the kitchen. Having forgotten to eat anything since last night's early dinner, the fuzzy light-headedness told her it was time to get something into her stomach.

Gripping the handle on the door to the refrigerator and reading the note she'd left for herself, it didn't initially make sense. "*You're in trouble?*"

Pulling the door open, she stepped back. "Yeah, I guess I am."

Two half-gallon containers of "100 Percent Florida Grown Orange Juice" and three packets of fast food hot sauce weren't what she was hoping to find. Looking through the clear glass into the fruit and vegetable drawers, they were as bare as the other four shelves.

Three glasses of mostly orange flavored sugar water and she was seated at her kitchen table with more questions than answers. First and most troubling was the problem going on in the city she had called home for the last year. How could this have happened so far from any of the facilities managed by BXF?

With the nearest base over five hundred miles to the north, it appeared unlikely that the two situations were related. She could attempt another call to Mr. Goodwin, although after the unusually awkward conversation they'd had earlier, she thought it better to wait a few days. If she were to get any definitive information from him, Emma needed to think through the conversation she intended to have a bit more before dialing.

If she had been relieved of her position at BXF, she would also need instructions on just how they wanted to transfer the responsibilities of the operation in Summer Mill. As far as she was aware, there were only a handful of people who even knew it existed. And those who did already had full-time positions.

"I need to call home."

Reaching for her cell phone and powering it on, she smiled. "Damn persistent, I'll give 'em that." Having missed another seven calls from Mr. or Mrs. Unknown, Emma was now more curious than irritated. And as she opened her favorites, with the intention of again trying to reach her brother, their timing could not have been better.

As the *Unknown Caller* again appeared across the top of the phone's display, Emma took a deep breath. "If this is a sales call, they're going to wish they never dialed this number."

Pressing Accept and then Speaker, she set the phone on the table in front of her. "HELLO?"

"Emma... Emma Runner?"

"Yes, this is Em—"

The voice on the other end cut her short before

she could finish. The man's gritty voice and near perfect diction told her he was either a news reporter, a politician, or possibly military. "Ms. Runner, we don't have much time, so I'm going to need you to listen very closely."

"Wait, who is this and why the hell have you called me like fifty times this morning?"

"My name is Richard Daniels, Major Richard Daniels. I'm a business associate of your former employer. Now, I need you to listen. I need you to do exactly as I say. No more and no less."

"Excuse me Major Daniels, but why on earth would I—"

The mystery man barked into the phone. "Look, there's no time for pleasantries. Haven't you seen the news this morning?"

"Yes, Los Angles is like a war zone, but I'm safely inside my home and don't plan on leaving any time soon. And not that it's any of your business, but I've also got a security team right outside."

"Emma, your former superior Marcus Goodwin is and always was a waste of human DNA. I know he ended your employment with BXF earlier this morning and want to help. Actually, I think we may be able to assist one another."

"Wait," Emma said as she grabbed her phone and walked into the living room. "Are you offering me a job?"

"Not exactly. This is something a bit more involved."

"Major Daniels, if that's even your real name, I

appreciate the phone call, but I've got some thinking to do. I'll tell you what, give me your number and once I get my career or what's left of it sorted out, I'll give you a call."

The man on the other end of the line paused before speaking. It sounded as if he was speaking under his breath to someone on his end, before abruptly coming back. "Emma, go your window and without making a big production out of it, check on your security detail."

"What?"

"Go do it, then we'll talk."

Back over to the bay window, she lowered the wood shutter just an inch and peered out into the street. The black SUV was gone. The space it occupied less than two hours earlier, as well as the street beyond, was much different than when she'd last walked through her front door.

She counted no less than two dozen people, some her neighbors, others unfamiliar. They appeared to struggle with the same affliction as the seniors from the news report earlier that morning. They shuffled without purpose from one driveway to the next, never focusing their attention on anything in particular. Their clothes were torn free in places, and most were marred with a thick burgundy glaze over much of their face and neck. Whatever this was had found its way into her neighborhood.

Out past her mailbox and across the street, her neighbor Melissa, a thirty-something mother of three, exited through an open garage door, apparently confronting those marching freely across her lawn. Her words were lost to Emma, although as the young mother waved her index finger and scolded a pair of wayward trespassers, she was backed into the driveway and taken down to the unforgiving concrete.

Turning away a half second too late, Emma pushed the shutters closed as the young woman's head burst open on impact. The disturbance caught the attention of others in the area and before she turned back to the phone, her neighbor fell victim to the ravenous crowd. As the flesh was torn away from her neck, shoulders, and torso, all that remained were the bone-chilling screams that brought others in around her.

"Major Daniels, what is happening?"

"Emma."

"Yes."

"All I can tell you is that the world is going to be a different place from now on. And this isn't just limited to Los Angeles, it's everywhere."

Her heart rate began to climb and her breaths were quick. "What do I do? Those men that brought me here are—"

"I know, they're gone," he said. "I also know that you've been cut off from BXF completely. Marcus Goodwin is pulling all his resources into the city for his own personal safety."

"You said you wanted to help. What do you need me to do?"

"I will send someone for you later this evening or

first thing in the morning. I have a secure location where I and a few others are going to ride this thing out. When we arrive there later today, I will send someone back for you."

"Later tonight," Emma said. "Or tomorrow?"

"I need to first make sure the place we're heading to is safe. And as long as you keep your windows closed and your lights off, you will be fine."

"Okay."

"Emma, I will call you again when we arrive. Do not leave your home before that. Charge your phone now and stay put. We aren't sure how long the power will stay on; it's already out in some areas."

"How will I—"

"Emma I have to go. Do you have a weapon in your home?"

"Yes, I have a handgun, but I haven't shot it in—"

"Good, keep it with you at all times. I will be in touch."

27

His left foot had gone numb within just the last five minutes. The volume in his right ear had also adjusted itself down to slightly above a whisper as the freezing wind pelted the exposed skin along half of his body. Griffin's lower back tightened as he dragged the second body away from the low-hanging blue spruce and laid it alongside the others.

They'd gotten to Cora, only seconds before he did, although without completely disrobing her, he couldn't be certain she hadn't been infected. Coagulated blood dried in dense patches along her face and then disappeared into the collar of her jacket. And as he pulled the black nylon away from her neck, four scratch marks traced a line from her clavicle into her armpit.

Dropping his hands into the snow, Griffin pressed a fistful of frozen flakes into Cora's wound. And as it melted into the warmth of her skin, he scanned the treeline for any additional pursuers.

"You've got to be kidding me," he said under his breath.

Wiping away the cracked trails of red that

covered the scratches brought him no closer to an answer. The unprotected skin near her bra strap had grown bright red from the extreme temperature change and seemed to antagonize the ambiguous scores backlit in red.

At his back, and judging from what he remembered of the topography, probably no more than twenty seconds off, something disturbed the rhythmic cadence of the storm. Without time to check his weapon, he recounted in his head the shots he'd taken since leaving the roadway.

Sliding the Glock into his waistband, he reached for Cora's left arm as she involuntarily lurched forward. Her eyes shot open as she screamed and reached for Griffin's face. Clutching her wrist and leaning forward, he used his free hand to push her leg up under her, and then tossed her onto his back. "Just keep quiet and hold on."

Cora continued to struggle against his tensed arms, as he stood from a squatting position and turned in the direction of the commotion not quite twenty yards back. "Will you just let me save your ass?"

Twisting back to center, Griffin fought the urge to run as he started downhill. Planning each step as he moved along the ice slicked hillside, he grew more confident with each new outcropping. As he settled into a rhythm, Cora had also realized their situation or had given into whatever was happening to her. Either way, she was now quiet and had stopped resisting.

As the sloshing footsteps at his back intensified, Griffin was unable to decipher his from theirs, and wouldn't be able to estimate their distance without stopping and turning. Left with no other options, he continued through the maze-like terrain and barked into the storm. "Cora."

She didn't initially respond, although he could feel her warm breath against the back of his bare neck, and that pushed him to increase his speed. She bounced lightly off his shoulders with each passing step and as he cut sharply to the left and pushed off the thick base of the frosted spruce, the centrifugal force pulled Cora's body in the opposite direction.

"Hey," she said. "What's going—"

"Hold on tight," Griffin shouted through labored breaths. "And tell me how close they are."

As he pushed his way through a dense patch of frozen juniper, the next glade, more than fifty yards from end to end, came into view. Stepping down into a bed of knee deep powder, Griffin's right foot shifted as it contacted a belt of ice covered shale, sending both he and Cora onto their backs.

Rolling over and onto his hands and knees, he reached for Cora and pulled her into his chest. The low branches in the gap between the dusted shrubs began to flit back and forth. Others were coming, although if they stayed hidden below the white deck, he and Cora may just have a chance. He only needed five minutes without the searing pain that blistered both his hands and his feet, just a few minutes to catch his breath.

Sliding down into the powdery refuge, he felt his internal temperature drop with each second that fell away. Whispering to Cora, they laid back against a compacted mound of snow as their bodies sat shoulder to shoulder. "Stay down. Let's give them a few minutes to scatter. I think I found our way out."

Now fully alert, Cora wrapped her hands around his and pulled them into her tattered jacket. "We're gonna die out here. Aren't we."

"No," Griffin said. "We're not."

Sliding closer, Cora pulled her right hand away momentarily and brushed the melting snow out of his hair. "I'm not even sure that we aren't already dead. Because I can't imagine hell being much worse than this."

Griffin laughed, but made sure to keep his volume contained to the three-foot cavern they presently occupied. "How's your side?"

"Numb."

"Your hands and feet?"

"Same," Cora said. "You?"

"I'll be fine. I guess it's a good thing I can't feel anything below my calves, because we're gonna need to run. You up for that?"

"I don't know," Cora said. "I guess."

"Okay, another sixty seconds and we go. We need to get way out in front of them so they lose our trail, so once we stand, we're not gonna look back. We're not gonna slow down and we're definitely not gonna stop, no matter what. Does that work for you?"

"Sure," Cora said. "I just hope my body agrees."

Turning to face her, Griffin said, "I know I said I didn't want to know anything about your past, but I have to ask one question."

Cora furrowed her brow and pulled in the corner of her mouth. "Okay?"

"I don't pretend to know much about where you and the others came from, but I'd always heard that the guards weren't allowed to carry weapons."

"They weren't. A few of them maybe had some pepper spray, but that was all."

"Got it... so why we're *those* guards carrying weapons?"

"I'm not sure, maybe they knew something we didn't."

"Maybe?"

28

Out of the alcove and into the hall, their massive childhood friend now rested comfortably in a heap, blood collecting around his oversized frame. Quickly moving around the body, Ethan was careful to avoid stepping directly into what remained of Franklin's obliterated head. Pausing, he nodded further into the hall, where three additional cots had begun to stir. "This is just getting ridiculous."

"Only fire your weapon if it's absolutely necessary," David said. "We may need to fight our way back out of here."

"Okay, so we're starting now, after you just sprayed Franklin's head all over the back half of the hospital?"

"You'd rather we fought him hand to hand?"

Ethan didn't respond. Taking the lead, he moved with a purpose and in a straight line through the two rows of cots. Pulling the sixteen-inch, expandable steel baton from his belt, he swung hard on whatever was attempting to rise from the third cot on the left. Adrenaline pushed him forward.

Not looking back to check his handiwork, he

stepped to the opposite row, twisted right, and brought the tempered steel down again. As the second shrouded body dropped back into place, Ethan increased his speed and cleared the transitory gauntlet in time to see his friend eliminate the third and final threat.

Reaching the corner, Ethan motioned to another set of double doors thirty feet ahead. "Through there, or you want to take the long way?"

"How's your shoulder."

"What?"

"Your shoulder," David said. "How's it holding up?"

"I think we have a decision to make here, and it has nothing to do with how you or I feel. I really don't think we have the time for this small talk."

"If we're going through that door, we'll need to fight. And if I have to do it alone, we're both dead. So, how's your shoulder?"

"You didn't just see me swing on those two back there? I'd say the only thing you need to worry about is yourself."

"We'll see about that, just try to keep up."

Ethan jumped first and was in a dead sprint before David had time to react. Reaching the set of doors, the pair moved to opposite sides of the corridor and leaned into the wall. Ethan rested his elbow against the panic bar and slowly pushed it in.

With the door opposite him parting only an inch, David bent forward and peered into the next hall. He nodded, looked back to Ethan, and held up both hands, five fingers from one and three on the other.

His back now against the door, Ethan gripped the baton. He waited as David slid to the right and mirrored his position. Pushing through the threshold first, Ethan stayed along the wall and side-stepped the first attacker.

Drawing his right arm back, he came around with the baton at full extension, striking the second walking corpse just below the temple. As he followed through and the metal rod skipped off the wall, Ethan lost his balance and fell forward into his next target.

Only a step behind, David continued his slow jog and used the blunt end of his weapon to push back the beast clawing at his friend. Reaching in before the situation escalated any further, he pulled Ethan back and stepping forward, kicked the feet out from under the man with half an arm.

Onto his feet, Ethan looked past David and quickly assessed the remaining twenty feet to the open cafeteria area. "Five more."

"Stay close," David said. "Were almost there."

Shoulder to shoulder, they slowed to a walk as the infected tourists moved to within fifteen feet. Ethan turned to his friend and spoke quietly. "How you wanna do this?"

"Two for you and three for—"

"Wait," Ethan said. Over his right shoulder, a single sliver of light filtered out into the hall from the cracked door to the hospital's main laundry room. He turned and before David could answer, disappeared behind the door.

As the crowd continued to close the gap, David let out a long whisper-shout. "EEEETTHHAANN!" Unfortunately, his voice carried through the extended hallway and into the cafeteria, gaining the attention of a second group of would-be aggressors.

Not more than a five feet away, David pulled his weapon and took two steps back. As the small horde continued forward, Ethan exploded through the swinging door, pushing a large laundry cart. "Let's go."

Out into the hall, Ethan plowed sideways into the small group of Feeders, instantly taking the first four to the ground. And as the momentum carried him into the opposite wall, the oversized plastic bin struck the last one just below the waist and flipped her into the bin. Struggling to stay upright himself, Ethan turned and headed for the cafeteria. "David, let's go."

The stout female, now flailing at the bottom of the cart, clawed at the slick plastic as Ethan continued pushing through the narrow hallway. Attempting to free herself, she managed to flip onto her back and was now face up, as David fell in alongside his friend.

The badly disfigured woman tore at the air and flailed against the momentum of the cart as the men looked down on her. "Do it," Ethan said.

David left one hand on the cart and with the other he reached into his belt and withdrew a six-inch folding knife. He quickly leaned in, drove the blade into the right side of her head, and pulled it back, her body motionless before he looked back at Ethan. "She was already gone."

Ethan stopped pushing and upon reaching the perimeter of the cafeteria, turned to his friend. "Was it hard?"

"No, it's them or us."

"I know you're right, but it still couldn't be easy to—"

"No," David said. "It was easy. It was easy because my fiancée is on the other side of that cafeteria and I'm not letting anyone or anything stop me from getting to her. These things, whatever they've become, drew the short stick today. For whatever reason, they're gone and from what I saw in those videos, they aren't coming after us to ask for help. It's too late for them, but not for us. Keep that in mind."

"Alright, let's go."

Pushing into the cafeteria, Ethan gripped the rounded handles and guided the sky blue cart toward the left wall. Scanning the room, he looked for the path of least resistance through the maze of upturned tables, discarded bodies, and the massive traffic jam of square-backed, stackable chairs. This is where the battle was lost.

From beyond the cash registers and alongside the destroyed breakfast buffet, another six Feeders stood and turned their way. Moving more quickly than the others they'd encountered thus far, the first pair to step out into the open were nearly running. Their unnatural, almost animalistic gait sent an icy tremor down the middle of Ethan's back.

Motioning toward the darkened hall at the opposite end of the room, and across twenty feet of stained white linoleum, Ethan looked back at David. "Is that where we're going, in there, through that mess?"

Again on the move, David turned and walked quickly backward as Ethan drove. "No other choice. But keep this bin between us and anything that comes our way."

Exiting the hall and converging with the group from the cafeteria, the growing horde of Feeders now numbered just over a dozen. As they turned their attention to Ethan and David, the pair bolted for the tangled web of tables at the center of the room.

Ethan stayed with the cart as David flanked right, attempting a shortcut. Keeping his friend in his periphery, he leapt a downed trash bin, dug in, and sprinted toward the opposite hall. Sidestepping an overturned display case and avoiding the bottles of water that had jumped from their home, he planted his left foot and leapt onto the first table.

His attention laser focused on the three offices just beyond the room, David's right foot came down atop a wayward serving tray, plastic on plastic. Sliding off the opposite end of the table, he found himself on his back, between a refrigerated soda machine and a decorative potted sago palm.

Pushing into a seated position, David flinched as he attempted to free himself. His right ankle had dropped between the table's legs and its vertical braces. And the awkward forward slant of the table made extracting himself impossible without help. His hand on his hip, he withdrew his weapon and pushed up under the table as far as the restricted space would allow.

With his friend rolling toward the scene, a small pack of Feeders had broken off from the main horde and started for him. They crossed the open space and had begun climbing the mountain of tables before Ethan slowed the bin and came in from the opposite end.

They would reach him well before Ethan; this was obvious. David could empty what was left in his weapon in an attempt to give himself a few extra seconds, although the next, much larger crowd would arrive just as Ethan did. He couldn't see any other way out of this. He and his best friend would end up dead, less than twenty feet from the woman he hoped to marry.

This new reality altered the game plan, but Carly was still his priority, no matter the cost. He wasn't willing to die at the hands and mouths of those things. He would fix this. "Ethan, go. Get the hell out of here. Find Carly and tell her I loved her."

David closed his eyes and placed the weapon to his head.

29

"On three we go, you ready?"

She wasn't. But the alternative, dying on this mountain, wasn't currently on her to-do list and she wasn't willing to make time for anything else. Trying to wiggle her toes, the pins and needles had moved from her forefoot up into her ankle and although she knew it wasn't a good sign, both feet had already gone numb.

"I'm good, I'll try to keep up." Peeking her head above the snowpack, Cora felt for the ridge of his shoulder and the pair stood in unison. She stayed close to his right arm as Griffin stepped heavily through the knee deep snow, both unwilling to focus on the threat at their backs.

The sounds of the forest had died down in the last five minutes, and although Griffin promised her he'd get her to the highway, Cora wasn't counting on it. They'd both watched as those hunting them weaved in and out of the frosted juniper, multiple times coming within feet of their miniature snow cave. Holding her breath became a ritual.

Glancing right as he kept moving, Griffin lowered

his head and spoke quietly. "There's one behind those trees. She knows we're here, but can't get to us until we break the treeline ahead."

Her breath rose from her mouth and crystalized as it lifted into the sky. "So, we're good, we'll make it to the road?"

Increasing his pace, Griffin moved out ahead and guided Cora left as he drifted right. "Yes, just keep moving toward the road. Once you reach the highway, point yourself downhill and keep going. I'll catch up."

Past the next clearing and not quite twenty-five yards from where the landscape bled into the roadway, something reflected what little sunlight fled the driving storm. Squinting, Cora was able to make out the color blue and a large swatch of chrome. Another ten paces and she realized what she was looking at. "Griffin."

He'd reached the treeline and had begun tearing free a branch nearly the size of a hockey stick when her voice reached him. Without turning, Griffin waved her off and moved to a tree more comparable in size to his own body.

Catching his breath, Griffin leaned into the narrow trail, checking the progress of their pursuer. As he brought the four foot limb overhead, his left shoulder hesitated. Bringing it back and to the side relieved the pressure from the decade-old injury as he counted down. "Five... four..."

Again Cora shouted his name, however, as she moved out away from the clearing, her voice was mostly lost to the trees. Continuing on, she began the descent and had disappeared from sight completely by the time Griffin finished counting down.

"Three... two... one..." Planting his trailing foot against the aging pine, Griffin twisted right and began to swing on the lonely Feeder. In the fraction of a second before making contact, the silence that befell the frozen utopia was extinguished.

Through the trees, across the expansive glade, and echoing from one valley to the next, a distant horn begged for attention. Following through, but with his focus being pulled away, Griffin struck the former prison guard just below the waist, snapping the branch in two.

Releasing the stick as his momentum carried him out onto the trail, Griffin continued forward and skidded face-first into the snow. Scurrying to his feet, he lunged for the broken branch and as his aggressor lay flailing on her back, he moved in. Dropping his knee onto her chest, he drove the larger of the two pieces into her right eye.

Back through the trees, he followed Cora's trail and the belligerent wailing, until he finally reached the edge of the glade. His lungs burned and his legs felt like two overcooked strands of linguini. Attempting to pinpoint the origin, he watched as thirty yards downslope, Cora stepped out of the forest and into the roadway.

Ten seconds behind her, Griffin navigated the rocky descent, focused entirely on staying upright and the placement of each labored step. He quickly traversed the rocky terrain and moved away from the trees. Reaching the asphalt, and stomping free the solidified ice and mud, he was again able to see the worn leather covering his frozen feet.

Following the hollowed footprints out across the four lane road, he spied Cora standing twenty feet from the source of the grating broadcast. The deep blue, late model pickup truck gathered snow along its roofline as it sat motionless, near the opposite side of the road. With no visible damage, it rested easily with its front bumper kissing the end post of the Walter Hamilton Bridge.

He stepped quickly through the slush and standing at Cora's side, shouted over the horn. "You see it hit?"

"No, it was sitting here before I walked out. But the horn... that just started."

Nodding, Griffin started for the driver's door as Cora followed. With his open palm against the window, he stepped back and wiped away the building frost. "Cora, get back." Stepping behind the cab, Griffin pulled his weapon and motioned for her to join him.

"What's wrong?"

"The driver's dead," Griffin said.

Turning to the sign at the side of the road, Cora said, "Let's go for help. It looks like the next town—Summer Mill—is only two miles up the road. My feet are already numb, so there's that."

"We're definitely going to Summer Mill, but we're not walking. I'm done with this freakin' weather.

We're taking this truck and driving out of this hellhole. Right now. We need to get you to the hospital, and get your side looked at."

"What about the driver?"

"He's gone."

"Are you sure?"

"Look," Griffin said. He again cleared the glass and motioned for Cora to come in close.

The driver, a balding forty-something male, was slumped forward, his forehead resting hard on the steering wheel—the apparent cause of the torturous horn assaulting their eardrums. Blood ran from his mouth, and his eyes were pinned in the open position. There were obvious signs of attack, as his throat and most of his neck were torn away, exposing the sinewy fibers securing his skull to his clavicle.

Bent at the waist, Cora peered through the driver's window and came to the same conclusion, although looking past the driver, she held her hand over her mouth and slowly backed away. "You're right, he is dead. But you missed something."

"What are you talking about?"

"He's not alone in there."

30

Allowing the plastic bin to drift into the hall, Ethan ran to the mountain of overturned tables. As he rushed past the first few, he could see David. The glass case near the wall reflected the image of his best friend, now raising the gun to his own head. Beyond that, a growing horde pushed into the small space alongside the vacant checkout lines.

As David's index finger slid down and met the trigger, Ethan rushed in behind the end of the slanted table. Gripping the left corner, he shouted. "David, no!" Without waiting for an answer, he lifted his end of the table up over his head, and started pushing toward the wall, the resistance much greater than he expected.

With the gritty sound of a joint being dislodged and the resistance falling quickly away, Ethan struggled to stay on his feet as David cried out, dropped the weapon, and grabbed at his right ankle.

The length of the table now vertical, and with it leaned into the refrigerated case, Ethan looked down on his friend. Positioned up against the wall, in the tightly spaced pocket created by a trio of upturned tables, David writhed in agony. "My foot, you idiot. What the hell was that?"

Ethan didn't answer. His friend was about to take his own life. Anything short of that was progress.

David's right foot was bent at an unfortunate angle and still attached to the table's vertical bracing, however he was now hidden on three sides by the makeshift barrier. And with little chance of the horde getting to him, Ethan stepped back, secured the upturned table, and withdrew his weapon.

Leaning in, Ethan bent down and looked through the one-inch void between the two tables. "I'm going for Carly, and taking these guys with me. I don't care what you have to do. Get free from that table and be ready to go in five. I'll carry you out myself if I have to. And I shouldn't have to say this, but that weapon is for them, not us."

Pushing away, Ethan stared at the crowd as he backpedaled. Finding an errant chair, he lifted it overhead and tossed it at them. "Let's go boys, come get it."

As the horde turned their attention away from the tables surrounding his friend, Ethan sprinted to the hall at the opposite end of the room. Passing the bin, he moved into the darkened corridor and started with the first office.

Locked door.

Coming to the second office, Ethan took a deep breath and turned the handle. The door slid open, but only a few inches. Lowering his shoulder, Ethan pushed against the obstruction and whispered into the blacked out office. "Carly?"

Nothing.

With both hands on the handle, Ethan leaned in and forced the door another eight inches. Glancing into the office, two lifeless bodies lay back to back. A brilliant white lab coat, painted in swatches of burgundy, was draped over the woman lying facedown. Her torso resting flush against the backside of the door prevented Ethan from entering.

Turning to door number three, time had run out. The horde from the cafeteria had entered the hall and two of the more agile Feeders had broken away from the pack. Ethan estimated he had five seconds to make a decision.

Gripping the handle of another locked door, he reached for his weapon, ready to fight his way back to his friend. He came here to find Carly, but not at the cost of David's life, or his own. If he lost the battle here in this place, where people came to heal, so would his best friend, and the woman somewhere in this desolate hospital.

David could perhaps hold out until another group of curious Feeders picked up his scent, and then maybe another five or ten minutes beyond that. But Ethan's timeline was a polar opposite. If he were to have a chance at living, any at all, the time was now.

Sighting his first target, Ethan let out a slow breath and squeezed the trigger. The disfigured corpse twisted violently to the left, smashed into the wall, and dropped face-first to the carpet. Lining up his second target, he took two steps forward and felt a rush of cool air against the right side of his face. Grabbed by the upper arm, he was pulled onto his heels and then backward off his feet.

Bracing for impact, Ethan released his grip on the nine millimeter. Crashing to the cheap commercial grade flooring, he slid through a doorway and into another body. Clawing to get to his feet, he was held back by two sets of hands, one atop his shoulders and the other around his waist.

Kicking through the confusion, a clammy, bloodstained hand dropped over his mouth as he was pulled backward, into the pitch black office.

With the door slammed shut, Ethan struggled against the forces holding him captive. His right arm throbbed, and as he tried to pull free, his shoulder discharged a wave of agony up through his neck and into the base of his skull.

Flat on his back, the intense pain played havoc with his vision, and as the hands released him, a soft desk lamp was powered on. "Ethan."

The smooth, pleasant voice belonged to her. His best friend's fiancée sat on her knees just two feet away. Her face was familiar, but now also different. Her shoulder length blond hair, matted and dirty, clung to her face in thick swatches. Her baby blue scrubs, bloodstained and torn, hung from her thin frame like an old dish towel. She forced a smile, her teeth barely visible, but Ethan knew better. "Carly."

"Ethan, where's David, where is he?"

"He's out there."

"Don't you tell me," she said, tears already forming near the corners of her eyes. "Don't you even try to—"

"No Carly; he's okay. His ankle is a bit busted up, but he'll be fine. I'm getting you out of here." Moving his gaze from Carly to the boy seated in the desk chair, Ethan continued. "Who the hell are you?"

Unfazed, the kid with a close-clipped buzz cut sat forward and smiled. "My name is Benjamin Westbrook, but you can call me Ben." The perfect smile, the high cheekbones, the build of a college athlete, this kid looked like he should be in Hollywood, and not cleaning trash cans at Summer Mill Memorial.

"What are you, like sixteen?"

"Twenty-three, but why does that matter to you?"

Ethan stood, took two steps forward, and punched Ben in the face, knocking the boy backward and out of the chair. "Ben, the next time you put your hands on me, you'd better be prepared to own it. You're old enough to know that you never put your hands on someone firing a weapon."

Moving to Ben, Carly looked up at Ethan and shook her head. "Really Ethan, he was just trying to help."

"Help?" Ethan said, as he moved in close. "He may have just killed us all. That weapon, the one that was going to get us out of the building, is now out there in the hall. And unless you're ready to open the door and go at those things bare-handed, I'd say he just screwed us."

Helping Ben to his feet, Carly handed Ethan a map of the building. "Where's David? Tell me exactly where you left him."

Unfolding the map, Ethan pointed to the spot where David sat encircled by the barricade of tables. "He's here. I have him blocked off by a few overturned tables. If we can create a distraction, just for a few minutes, I can pull him free and we can all get out through the back door." Looking up at Ben, he said, "I just need some help."

"I'm fast," Ben said. "Like really fast. I can lure them away from the cafeteria, then you and Carly can get to David and meet me in the back hall."

Ethan looked to Carly. She nodded, grabbed the red backpack from the desk, and slung it over her left shoulder. "He really is fast, it may just work."

"Okay," Ethan said. "No rehearsals. David needs us now. I'll open the door, you make a break for the other side of the kitchen and we'll go for David. Meet you on the other side, you good?"

Ben smiled, his left eye beginning to swell. "Let's do it."

Ethan gripped the door handle, and turned to the kid. "Hey, no hard feelings?"

Rolling his neck from left to right, Ben ignored Ethan's olive branch. He instead turned to Carly and wrapped her in his lengthy arms. "We're getting out of here, all of us." His focus back on the door, Ben stood ready for Ethan to make his move.

Ethan stepped back, opened the door, and moved out into the hall. Coming to the first threat, he shifted his weight to his trailing leg and kicked the first Feeder backward and into the wall. Continuing forward and reaching for his weapon, he grabbed a handful of nothing as Ben swept in from the right, snatched the weapon, and continued running.

As Ben sprinted toward the end of the hall, catching the attention of the horde, Ethan grabbed Carly's hand. "When we get out of here, I'm probably going to kill that kid."

31

Running back through the plan in his mind, Griffin watched the woman in the passenger seat thrash about under the restraint of her tightly wound seatbelt. Shards of her husband's flesh hung from her mouth as she lurched forward, shredding the skin along the right side of his body.

Griffin moved to the bed of the truck, and rifling through the couple's newly purchased camping gear, located a ten-inch cast iron skillet, two ultra-compact waterproof flashlights, a twenty-six inch camper's axe, and a four-person extreme weather easy-pitch tent. He reached for the axe, turned to Cora, and motioned to the opposite side of the road. "Take my gun, if she gets past me... shoot her."

Shouting over the horn, Cora said, "You want me to do what?"

"We have to get them out of there somehow, and I'm not going to pull him out of the driver's seat with her trying to rip my face apart."

"Hey," Cora said, "It looks like the snow's slowing down."

"Yeah, but we're still taking this car."

"Okay, but I'm not too sure about—"

"Just stand there and be ready." Griffin gripped the door handle and paused for a second, the metal cold in his hand. Lifting the handle he quietly slid the door open and stepped back. As the driver's corpse tilted left, and then dropped face-first into the road, the horn assaulting the entire valley finally died a quick death.

Pacing the shoulder, Cora intermittently checked the treeline at her back for stragglers from the previous accident, listening to the whispers of the forest. Attempting to get a glimpse of his progress, she marched toward the bridge and looked past Griffin. "You okay?"

He didn't answer. Instead he hooked the axe blade under the man's right leg and pulled his lower half out onto the asphalt. And with the woman still belted into the passenger's seat, Griffin stepped over the driver to get a better vantage.

Her face contorting, she growled from the back of her throat and clawed at the seat next to her. She was beautiful, well at least she was before whatever this was happened to her. Griffin quickly spotted the multiple bite marks along her wrists and arms, most having already turned a shade darker than black. However, her face was virtually untouched, save for the trails of dried blood that had run from her chin and disappeared into her destroyed fleece pullover. Continuing to writhe, the woman peered into Griffin's eyes, and begged to be released.

Stepping back, he turned to Cora. She was

momentarily occupied with checking the trees, but quickly spun back, realizing he had been staring at her. "Okay," she said. "Let's go."

"Almost, but I need you to be ready. Are you ready?"

"Yes, but I think there are a few of them from the bus still out there."

"That's why we need to get this done quickly."

Cora didn't answer, she instead gave Griffin a thumbs up and then pressed her hand back into her hip. With the barometer rising, the numbness brought on by the arctic temperatures began to subside. She hadn't yet told him, but the wound along her left flank again began to ooze.

Without the space to take a full swing at the seated passenger, Griffin pushed the door open to its limit and then used the axe to carefully depress the red button on the seatbelt buckle.

As the belt retracted into its housing, the wiry female launched through the driver's door, as if strapped to a rocket. As Griffin stepped to the left and swung the axe, he missed. Instead, his elbow glanced the left side of her face, sending her into his legs, and both of them to the ground.

Up to her knees, she was much faster than the others. As Griffin scrambled to retrieve the axe, she'd locked onto his scent. Crawling on all fours, she reached for his pant leg and took a boot to the face. As she came again, Griffin attempted to stand, but slipped on a small patch of black ice, and before he could recover, she'd leapt onto his back.

From the edge of the road, Cora ran in, weapon in hand. As the deranged beast pulled at the collar of his jacket, attempting to get to his face and neck, she raised weapon. "Griffin, move."

From below the woman, he turned to see Cora raise the nine millimeter pistol and extend her arms. Gritting his teeth, Griffin closed his eyes and tensed every muscle from the waist up. As the gun exploded, the woman's face dropped onto the back of his neck. He instinctively rolled to the left, sending the woman back onto the roadway.

Griffin reached for the axe, and standing over his aggressor, drove the blade deep into the charred chasm created by the exit wound in her forehead. Incensed, he stuck her again, and again. He'd driven the stainless steel blade into her face more times than he could count, and as his arms and hands began to cramp, Cora stepped in slowly and laid her hand on his back.

"She's gone... We have to go, right now."

Shaking free from his rage-induced haze, Griffin followed Cora to the truck and climbed into the driver's seat. She let him take the lead and moved to the passenger side. Sliding in, she shut her door and asked him to do the same.

With one eye on the rearview mirror, Cora watched as another frozen corpse walked out from behind the tall spruce, and then into the road. "Griffin, let's go."

Glaring through the windshield, he reached down, felt for the keys. Noticing it was left in drive, he gave the keys a quarter turn, shifted into park, and restarted the truck. Backing away from the end post, he pointed to the sign she'd noticed earlier. "Summer Mill. That's where we part ways. I'll get you help, then I'm leaving."

"Griffin, what are you taking about? I thought—"

"What'd you think? That we'd ride off in the sunset together? Really you? Me? And after you almost blew my head off out here? I somehow don't see it."

"You're kidding right?" Anger beginning to drive the volume in Cora's voice. "I saved your ass back there. If I hadn't shot her when I did, you'd be dead right now, or worse, you be lying next to that man with half your face eaten off. And somehow you don't see that. Well, good luck then."

As the slow-paced former detainee continued toward the truck, Griffin shifted into drive and started across the bridge. Reaching into the console, he grabbed a hand drawn map and held it on the steering wheel, between his hands. "This is where they were headed. Poor guy probably thought he could get her help."

"So, that's it?" Cora said. "We're done discussing what happened out there? Why, because of what you thought happened?"

Griffin slammed the brake to the floor. "Yes, you got lucky. But the bullet that tore through her head, also came damn close to doing the same exact thing to me. Too damn close. Maybe it's my fault though, maybe I shouldn't have even handed you the gun in the first place, and it's obvious you can't—"

"Griffin, just drive the damn truck, you're beginning to sound like an ignorant fool. What you don't know, not that it matters, is that I've had a weapon in my hand since before I could walk. I've seen you shoot out there and let's just say I could show you a thing or two. It's just too bad you're throwing me out once we get to town. Oh, and by the way that round, the one that you think came too close... it actually entered her head exactly where I planned."

Not responding directly to her explanation, Griffin handed her the hand drawn map. "We're going to Summer Mill Memorial, the same place it looks like he was taking her. I'll need you to give me directions."

Cora set the piece of eight and a half by eleven in her lap. "Griffin, you saved my life out there this morning, maybe more than once, and for that I'm eternally grateful. But you also wouldn't be sitting her right now if I hadn't taken that shot, so I'd say we're about even. I think you need to get used to the idea of accepting help from others, because you're going to need it."

32

Sitting alone in the corner of her bedroom, daylight filtering in through the wood shutters, Emma pushed aside the Project Ares file and reached for the brightly colored photo album. This, the only personal possession she'd thought to take in the hasty move to Los Angeles, was now her only connection to the family she so desperately needed.

Emma gazed at the handmade cover, not knowing if she'd ever again get to see the people staring back at her. Her mother, her father, Ethan—they were only two dimensional beings now. The things she remembered, she was likely to someday forget. The way her mother's baked potato soup tasted after a long hot shower. Her father's awful jokes. How her big brother always kept one eye on her, but would never admit to it. She wanted to go to them, to see them, to sit with them, to laugh, to cry. But, for now, she could only look through the memories.

Opening the album, she'd flipped to a pair of photos from her freshman year in high school. She stood alongside her mother and father. Three smiles, each bigger and more contrived than the next.

Within hours of taking the top spot in the Colorado State Science Fair, the day couldn't have ended better. A defining moment that led to a string of four consecutive state titles, a moment that would end with acceptance to four Ivy League schools, and define who she'd be as an adult. A special time that almost never happened. Her brother, the only one not pictured, was the reason.

.   .   .

At exactly sixteen minutes before four o'clock, on September 22nd, 1995, it hit her. Not like a ton of bricks, but more like the eighteen wheeler carrying the bricks. Emma sat in the corner of the conference hall, searching her three plastic bins for the vial containing the homemade anticoagulant. Staring up at her parents who'd just arrived, tears began to roll down her fourteen-year-old face.

Her mother tried to comfort her as best she knew how, and her father only asked why she couldn't present her findings without the missing vial. She just cried.

"Hey." Ethan appeared from the opposite end of the hall. Fresh from football practice, and wearing his best pair of slacks, his grin began to fall as he saw her face. "Did you lose already?" His jokes were usually well received. This one wasn't.

Her father turned and shook his head. "She's missing something, says she can't even present without it."

Looking to his mother and then to Emma, he said,

"What is it and why can't you get another one?"

Fishing through her bins yet again, hoping for the missing item to somehow reappear, she looked back at her brother. "I had this. My research could have actually helped people, you know someday. Now I'm done. Mrs. Amhurst is going to kill me. I told her about it, but never showed her the actual results. I have no proof this even works."

"Can't you just show her tomorrow?" Ethan was trying, but it just wasn't enough.

"No, I'll probably fail the class, and she has a few friends here from the university that are expecting to see my presentation. I'm going to make her look bad too."

Her mother began digging through the third bin, not even knowing what she was looking for. "You didn't have any extra?"

"Yes, mom. But it's in the cooler in my bedroom, and my bedroom is at home. With the snow, it would take way too long to drive there and back. I'm already supposed to be—"

Ethan interrupted. "That nasty red cooler in the corner of your bedroom?"

"Yes, but—"

Turning and running toward the rear of the auditorium, Ethan said, "Start setting up, I'll be back in twenty minutes."

Her brother, in his senior year of high school, gave her a gift that she would remember every day for the rest of her life. He ran through miles of snow, half the time carrying a three-pound cooler, and arrived back at the convention center in just under thirty minutes.

Realizing there wasn't enough time for his father to safely navigate the snowy five-mile route in the family car, Ethan reacted. He left through the rear of the auditorium, ran across the school yard, the snow-covered football field, and then leaping the rear wall, made quick work of the next six blocks.

The jog back was a different story. Not knowing the fragility of the cooler's contents, he slowed his pace, as not to add to the horrific day his sister was already amassing. Keeping the red rectangle upright, he matched nearly two-thirds of his original pace on the return trip, only once coming close to losing it all.

Marching into the auditorium, his sister again in tears and his mother nearly as angry as worried, he walked onto the stage and set the container by Emma's feet. He then leaned over, put his frozen, bright pink face next to her ear and said, "You're my sister. I love you. Please win this thing."

And she did.

Walking down the set of four steps and away from the presentation area, Ethan moved to the front row. Dripping ice cold beads of water out onto the grey linoleum floor, he sat and watched as his sister began to create her place in this world. Her ultimate contribution wouldn't be seen for another nineteen years, although as she replayed it, that day more than any, was the happiest she could recall.

.   .   .

Tracing her index finger over each of her family members, Emma closed her eyes and tried to imagine that they were somewhere safe. That they weren't scared and that they weren't alone. She prayed that she'd see them again and that they'd never be apart. She also hoped that a little part of Ethan's former self still existed. With everything that was happening out there, she knew he'd need it.

Setting the album atop the Project Ares file, Emma reached for her phone. Pressing the home button, the charge read ninety-seven percent. Sliding it open, she moved to the messages app and waiting for it to load, stared at her closed bedroom door.

Two new text messages. Both from her mother. As she went to open the first, her phone rang.

Major Richard Daniels.

With her phone still connected to the charger, Emma moved up onto her bed. "Hello?"

"Emma, you need to be ready to move in the next five minutes. I have someone in the area that will bring you here tonight."

"Major Daniels, I don't mean to sound ungrateful, but given the fact that we've never met and today is the first time I've ever even spoken to you, can you tell me where it is you want to take me?"

"I don't have much time to explain, but let's just say that this is a place that you would have ended up at someday. Your special skill set has all but assured that. Where you are going isn't what's important.

What is important is that we get you here in one piece. And just to put your mind at ease, this place is going to survive what's out there, and once you're behind these walls, you'll be able to breathe easy."

"But—"

"Listen, I haven't called to beg. If you've got a better offer, just say so. If not, take only what you can carry and go to your garage. My men will be pulling into your driveway within minutes. They'll come around to the side door and knock twice. You'll want to let them in." Major Daniels paused. "You still want to do this on your own?"

"No," Emma's hand began to shake. "I'll be ready to go."

33

Rounding the corner into the main dining area, David came into view. Pulling Carly in close, they leaned into the wall, and watched as Ben sprinted across the cafeteria floor and into the kitchen. Gaining the attention of a second, and much larger, group of Feeders, the kid was actually serving a purpose.

Moving on their hands and knees through the twisted mess of tables, Ethan and Carly reached the barricade protecting her fiancé. Through the vertical void between two of the barriers, they could see that David had freed his ankle and now appeared to be nursing another injury along his right arm.

Turning to Carly as he came to stand, Ethan held his index finger over his lips and whispered. "Remember, we're trying to be invisible. But, once I move this table, we may get some company."

"Okay?"

"Stay close, David's gonna need help. I'll get him out, but I need you to see what we don't. You ready?"

Ethan pushed his back into the wall and gripped the long edge of the table. His left leg braced against the floorboard and with David now aware of his presence, he began to slide the table away and to the right.

The gap growing, he asked Carly to stay at his back as he moved in and helped David to his feet. "Watch for Ben. As soon as he comes back through this room, we're going in the opposite direction. Let him lead them away, and we'll have a shot at getting to the back door."

Onto his feet, David winced. He pulled his right foot off the ground and hopped the three steps to Carly. Coming together, they embraced and began to kiss, clinging to one another for support. Pulling her in close, David whispered into her ear and looked back to Ethan for their next move. "What's with Ben?"

"You know that kid?" Ethan asked.

"We met him last night, you don't remember?"

"I don't know, I'm still a little fuzzy on what even happened this morning."

"So, are we just running out the back door?"

"That's the plan," Ethan said. "As soon as the kid comes by, we'll head through the back hall and hopefully the parking lot is clear. How many rounds you got left?"

"I don't know five, maybe six. Why, where'd yours go?"

"Your buddy, the track star. He took it."

"What?"

"Long story. But I'll tell you what, that boy is gonna know my name before this day is through. He picked the wrong person to screw with."

As the tide of Feeders followed Ben back out of the kitchen and across the cafeteria floor, Ethan leaned under David's right arm. He pointed to the last few Feeders filtering out of the swinging doors. "Carly, stay on my back. Hold on and don't let go. We go as soon as those last two clear the area."

Carly fell in behind Ethan, her hand shaking uncontrollably as she clutched his utility belt. As they started across the floor, Ethan allowed the tables to slowly crumble into themselves. The sound of metal on metal rumbled through the well-insulated room, sending riotous soundwaves down each of the four corridors.

"Come on." Ethan's head on a swivel, they crossed the floor with David doing his best to keep up. Reaching the archway leading into the rear hall, Ethan guided his friends to the second recessed doorway and stopped. "I'll go check it out. Don't move."

Without the use of his sidearm, he descended the darkened hall, quickly making his way to the set of double doors. From a squatting position and his back against the wall, he slowly leaned in and parted the doors. Just as they'd left it, the last fifty feet were a mess of metal-framed cots and further along, what remained of Leslie Franklin.

Back to David and Carly, Ethan was nearly out of breath. "Same as before... but."

"But what?" David said.

"A few of the cots are now empty. And I don't see

any of them back there."

"So, that's good."

"Okay, but where'd they go?"

"Who—"

Four shots in rapid succession detonated from the far end of the hospital. And then another three seconds of silence before the thundering clap of shattering glass.

Ethan pointed into the half lit corridor. "Now."

David had already begun to hobble in the direction of the doors as Ethan matched his pace and offered his shoulder. "No Ethan; I got it. Just watch the rear."

Traversing the two long rows of cots, Carly held David's hand and stayed as close to center as was possible. Maintaining eye contact with her fiancé, she avoided looking down and the thoughts that would come with allowing her mind to focus on anything but survival. She only wanted another twenty seconds. Just to get to the end. Through the rear doors and away from this hell. *Please, just please.*

Four steps behind, Ethan again turned and without a hint of what had become of the kid, he began to slow. He let David continue on toward the last set of double doors, leading Carly past their childhood friend and what was left of the annihilated corpse.

"Three..." Ethan waited.

Reaching the exit, David and Carly stopped and paused at the threshold. "Let's go, Ethan."

"Two... come on Ben." Ethan stared back in the

direction they'd come. "I'll leave you here, I swear."

Standing near the center of the aisle of death, something at his back stirred. Ethan knew what it was, but didn't turn. Two, maybe three new foes, struggling to free themselves from under the thin layer of hospital bedding. He was semi-confident in his ability to handle himself one-on-one and out in the open against these things, but he wasn't ready to die for the kid who'd just run off with his only advantage. It was time to go.

"One... Damn it kid, I'm sorry."

34

Twenty minutes since leaving the bridge in their rearview mirror, and without another human crossing their path, their world seemed much bigger than the mountain they'd fought to leave. Griffin had attempted conversation three times, partly because he hated absolute silence, but mostly because he felt something he didn't know what to do with. Something that typically he shoved aside. Guilt wasn't his thing, but maybe today it was.

The nine millimeter sat on the bench seat, dividing the cab into equal parts. Griffin behind the wheel, and Cora alternately staring at the map and out into the midafternoon sky. "Looks like we're coming up on Third Street. Turn left and then look for Mineral Street."

"Okay," Griffin said. "How's your side?"

"It's fine. I'll live."

He hated this. She came as close to blowing his head off as she did saving his life. And from where he sat, that fact was crystal clear. He believed he had every right to react the way he did and then some. And at some point she was going to see that, no matter how long it took him to convince her. "How are we going to handle the questions?"

Cora continued to peer out the opposite window.

"Hey, this is something we have to talk about. I'm still not asking for details about your past, but—"

"Well, then don't."

"It's not that."

Folding the map and laying it on the dashboard, Cora straightened up, loosened her seat belt, and turned to face him. She flashed a sarcastically-fake grin and said, "What—what is it that you think WE need to discuss? What kinds of things are you hoping that I tell you? Are you trying to find out what heinous act put me behind bars, or are you simply trying to apologize for acting like a child?"

"Neither. I just figured that we may want to get our stories straight as far as where we came from and you know, who we are."

"This isn't a movie." Cora said. "We aren't going to give them some fake story about who we are, have them patch up my side, and then just walk right out the front door."

"I realize that, but with everything—"

"Like you said earlier, you're going to drop me off and get back to your life. I'm going into the hospital and telling them exactly what happened back there. I've got less than six months left on my sentence and I'm not going to screw that up. Hell, life inside is a cake-walk compared to what we've been through the last few hours."

"I'm not leaving you. I'll stick around to make

sure they know what happened out there, and to make sure they know that you never tried to—"

"Tried to what, escape?"

Growing tired of the direction this one-sided conversation was heading, Griffin shook his head. "That's not what I was saying, I just—wait, what the hell is that?"

She began to respond, but seeing that his focus had moved away from the cab of the truck, Cora instinctively reached for the weapon that separated the front seat. Even before she was fully turned, the movement from three hundred yards away was undeniable.

Slowing the truck, Griffin pointed toward the end of Mineral Street. "See that big blue sign, white lettering?"

"Yeah?"

"That's the hospital, that's where we're going."

Counting the number of tortured individuals flooding the streets, she stopped when she reached twenty-five. As Cora held her breath, the roadway beyond Fourth Street disappeared into a sea of bodies. Men, women, and even a few children were gathered in small groups along the east end of Mineral. They walked in massive circles, each autonomous from one another. "There is no way we're going over there."

Pulling to a stop, Griffin leaned into the steering wheel. Squinting into the distance, he focused on the massacre that was about to take place in less than thirty seconds. "Do you see that?"

"Yeah, I do. What does that look like, maybe a few hundred? Do you think this is where it started? Is this the reason we almost died out there on that mountain?"

"No, look over there, that guy. He's running from them—no, over there on the right. There's actually someone still alive out there." Griffin shifted into drive and pushed the gas pedal to the floor. "We've got to get to him before they do."

"Griffin, no."

Pushing the truck toward the crowd, Griffin kept one eye on the unidentified runner as he turned the corner and moved into the hospital's employee parking lot. The young man appeared to be carrying a handgun and was closely pursued by more than a dozen of the dangerously aggressive individuals.

Dropping the magazine from the bottom of the nine millimeter, Cora looked back at Griffin. "Not good."

Arcing wide and aiming for the center of the drive, Griffin continued to track the unusually speedy individual. With each aggressor he was able to run away from, he would unfortunately find another three to join in the attack. At present, the young man was attracting more of the ridiculously enthusiastic followers than he was losing.

"What's not good?" Griffin asked.

"One gun, only two rounds left. We can't help him."

"We have to try."

Bracing herself against the passenger door, Cora

slid the gun under her left leg and held tight to the seatbelt. Only seconds from reaching the young man, now running in a straight line toward the employee entrance, the pain along her left side returned with a vengeance. Lurching forward as Griffin weaved between the slower moving individuals, she vomited onto the floorboard.

Finally gaining the attention of the young man with the gun, Griffin pointed the truck at those closing in on the rear entrance. "Cora, I'm sorry, but I have to do this—hold on."

Steering the truck into the crowd, the front end pitched forward. Going airborne, the engine throttled wildly as Griffin shot from his seat and collided with the roof. Leveling more than a half dozen aggressors, the truck came to rest alongside the emergency parking lane and rocked from left to right.

The man with the gun had momentarily disappeared. Although ten seconds later, he reappeared twenty yards away, darting out from behind a decorative stone column. His hands in the air, the young man locked eyes with Griffin and began to shout, although his words were masked by growl of the engine.

Shifting into reverse, Griffin looked through the rear window, and punched the gas. The truck's back end fought to gain traction as he searched for a clear route away from the mayhem. As the right rear tire gripped the asphalt, the massive vehicle shot backward and into a handicapped parking sign.

"Perfect."

Before she could compose herself, a second wave of nausea hit, this time accompanied by a thunderous spike that ended behind both eyes. A migraine so powerful that it threatened to rip her skull in two. The pain had taken control now, nothing for her to do but let it come. Just endure, somehow.

"Cora, just hold on a minute longer. Please." Dropping the truck back into drive, he plowed his right foot down onto the gas pedal and without warning, the engine died.

With long beads of sweat beginning to form along her forehead, Cora placed both hands on the dashboard and looked out over the side view mirror. "Griffin, they're coming for us—all of them."

35

Curiosity ate away at her until she finally moved back through the kitchen and into the living room. Kneeling near the window, Emma parted the wood blinds just enough to see the area beyond her front yard. There were fewer of those things moving about, although there were also no signs that anyone with a pulse still occupied the area.

Normally, her street was home to more cars than it could comfortably handle. Parked end to end, her neighborhood, most days, resembled a used car lot. The innate ability to parallel-park almost certainly should have been a prerequisite for purchasing a home along Taft Avenue.

Making multiple trips to the neighborhood at all times of the day, she insisted on a two-car garage. One of only three homes on the street to offer that luxury, she commended herself on the forethought. The daily crusade to locate a parking spot wasn't a battle she was willing to fight. Today was different for many reason, although the visual was off-putting. More people than vehicles. But not really people at all.

Back through the house, she made her way into the bedroom. The photo album was the first to be packed into the bottom of her oversized duffel, followed by the Project Ares file. Next were three pairs of jeans, four t-shirts, a zippered hoody, a wool beanie, four bras and every pair of panties she owned. How do you pack for a trip you know absolutely nothing about?

Slinging the black BXF duffel over her shoulder, she grabbed a second, smaller bag which contained her wallet, passport, identification, and the pistol Major Daniels had asked her about. Past the second bedroom, and into the garage, her stomach growled. Reminded that she hadn't eaten anything in nearly twenty-four hours, she set her bags on the cool concrete floor and started for the kitchen.

Reaching the archway between the hall and the front room, the sound of a vehicle skidding into the driveway pulled Emma away. She ran through the house and moved back into the garage as a car door slammed. Boots on the ground and then the side gate opening. Quick, quiet voices could be heard beyond the side door as Emma rushed over.

"Hello?" she said.

"Emma Runner, we've been sent by—"

Pulling open the door, two men. One tall, light skinned, and bald. The other, average height, build, complexion, and without any distinguishing features, except the tribal tattoo extending nearly an inch above his thick black turtleneck.

The tall man manufactured a hasty smile and held

out his hand, ready to take her duffel. "My name is Bret, this here is Chad. We'll be assisting you today. But we must go now."

"Sure, okay." Handing the oversized duffel to her new best friend Bret, she reached for her purse and followed the men to the side gate. Reaching the driveway, another gentleman sat behind the wheel of the light silver Hummer H2, staring into the rearview. From the shoulders up he was dressed much the same as the other two, and even through the windshield, held an air of absolute confidence.

The man who called himself Bret held open the rear passenger door as three of those things from the street took notice. And as Emma reached in to set her bag on the seat, her empty right hand looked out of place. "Wait," Emma said. "I have to go back."

Attempting to move away, she was caught from behind. Bret, the larger man with an astonishing reach, held her by the arm. "Ms. Runner, we're leaving. There isn't time for anything else."

Struggling to free herself, Emma pulled away. "My phone, it's still on the charger in my back bedroom."

Stepping into her path, Bret said, "It's too late. We must go now."

The other two men shouted from the interior of the Hummer as Emma stood her ground. "I'm going back for it, you can leave without me if you have to."

Scanning the street and the potential threat, Bret shook his head. "Ms. Runner, we've risked quite a bit coming here, please—just get in the back. There really isn't time."

"No," Emma said. "I'm not going without my phone."

"I don't think you understand, Ms. Runner, I meant exactly what I said. If you stay here, you will die. There really isn't a choice."

Again shaking her head, Emma said, "*You* don't understand. The only connection I have to my family is on that phone. You can let me go get it, or you can leave."

Looking past the oversized SUV, Bret placed his hand over the weapon protruding from his hip. "I'll get it for you. Tell me where it is, get in the vehicle and I'll go after it. That's your only option, and it has to happen right now."

"Okay," Emma said. "Back bedroom, straight in from the garage. It's sitting with the charger on the nightstand." Handing over her keys and sliding into the back seat, she closed the door.

Placing her bag on her lap, she turned to thank the tall man, but he was already gone. Faint footfalls disappeared along the side of the house and as the driver backed into the street, he yelled, "Brace yourselves."

Maneuvering through a backwards U-turn, the driver seemed impressed with himself, as he punched the gas, and slid backward into nearly the same spot he'd occupied moments earlier. Turning to the average-looking man in the passenger seat, he said, "You wanna take care of those two?"

"Let's give him a minute. I don't want to draw any unnecessary attention our way if we don't have to."

The driver laughed. "Yeah, like this morning. I still can't believe you two made it out of there in one piece."

More concerned with the crowd that had begun to form across the street from her driveway, Emma moved to the center of the bench seat. "Can I ask you guys something?"

"Sure, Ms. Runner," said the driver.

"Do you guys have any idea what all this is? That man, Major Daniels, he said this is happening everywhere. Was he serious?"

Mr. Average with the neck tattoo turned in his seat. "Yes he was. We've had reports that it goes as far away as—"

Banging at the rear window and then the door flying open, Bret was back. He slid in next to Emma and set the phone and charger down on the seat. "Go, Go, Go. We've got company on the next block, and it isn't going to be pretty. We may have to get out and fight these things."

The man behind the wheel shifted into drive, slammed his foot down onto the gas pedal, and turned right out of the driveway. "Where am I going? Back the way we came?"

"No," Bret said. "Go left at the corner and then take the first right after the torched van. We'll pick up Central after the freeway—if we make it that far."

Emma buckled her seat belt and turned to Bret. "Thank you."

"Don't thank me just yet; I still have a job to do."

As the SUV sped away from her home, she

powered on her phone and pulled up her messages. Still no communication from her brother. Instead of sending another wasted text message, she decided to call. Leaning away from Bret, she pressed the phone to her right ear and waited.

Voicemail.

"Ethan, please. I need you to let me know somehow, that you're okay. I got a few weird texts from mom this morning and I think maybe her and dad need some help. I'm back in California now, so please let me know—"

Brakes locking, and the squeal of warm rubber gripping the roadway forced her attention through the front windshield. As the Hummer relented to its own forward momentum, Emma tightened her grip around the phone, pulled her legs to her chest, and instinctively held her breath.

As the Hummer slammed into the sea of bodies that filled the far left lane of Central Avenue, Emma rebounded against the constricted belt, as Bret was launched from his seat. Gliding forward through the hailstorm of shattered glass, the large man somehow slipped through the void between the two front seats and came to rest atop the center console.

Her world went silent and although Emma didn't remember hitting her head, the goose egg rising from her left temple told her otherwise. She winced as she leaned forward, and grabbing the collar of Bret's black blazer, she strained to pull him back. Impossible. "Bret... Chad?"

No response.

Sitting back and looking down at her phone, the call to her brother had already ended. And glancing out through the shattered windshield, she watched as the horribly disfigured crowd descended on the front half of the embattled SUV.

Ethan, I hope you've made it somewhere safe. I love you.

36

Ben was there at the door and then he was gone. He'd led the horde away from the building and then returned. He still carried the weapon he'd taken from Ethan and didn't appear to be slowing down. He was back now, and as David leaned against the wall, Carly shouted down the empty hallway. "Ethan, come on. Ben's outside, we have to go."

Already running when he came through the door, Ethan moved quickly to his friend. Against the wall, he stood at David's side and reached for his right arm. "You ready?"

Removing the sheets he'd tied around the double doors, David pointed out into the lot. "I'm fine, I can walk. But we have another problem."

As Ben moved in through the doors, still attempting to catch his breath, Ethan stared out past the handicapped parking at the stationary truck. "What's this?"

Ben began to speak, but was quickly shut down by Ethan, who grabbed the much smaller man by the throat. "I'm not dealing with you just yet, but I will. Stay the hell out of my way, and I might just let you slide on the ass kicking you have rightly earned."

"But," Ben said.

"Not now." Leaning in, Ethan pulled the nine millimeter from his hand, checked the magazine, and slid it back into its holster. Now turning to Carly, he said, "Who are they?"

"We don't know. They flew into the parking lot just as we saw Ben running this way. They drove their truck over a whole lot of those things and then backed up and got stuck, right where they are now."

"We helping 'em?" Ben asked.

Carly turned to Ethan and tightened the straps on her backpack. "We have to, we can't just leave them out there."

"Okay, the kid and I will go get them, and you and David get to our truck. We're all leaving together."

David nodded in agreement. "Let's go."

His hand on the younger man's shoulder, Ethan said, "Can you still run?"

Ben nodded.

"Okay, stay on my right shoulder. If we get jammed up, you take off and lead them toward the back of the parking lot. I'll get whoever's in that truck out and away. We'll meet at the armored truck over there." To David and Carly he said, "Give us some time to draw them away, then go wide and don't stop for anything—no matter what happens."

Carly took David's hand and stood behind Ethan. They waited as the last few Feeders moved away from the building and joined the group moving toward the curious blue pickup. She rested her head on his shoulder and whispered, "We're together now. Let's keep it that way, okay?"

As he watched Ethan and Ben walk off around the right end of the crowd, David hugged his bride-to-be. "That's all I've ever wanted." And with the massive stone column temporarily shielding them from the eyes of the horde, David took Carly's hand and started for the truck.

Maintaining a decent pace, his limp was now nearly undetectable. Alongside Carly, he continued to eye the growing crowd as more spilled out of the street and into the rear lot. Thirty feet from the armored vehicle, he stared straight ahead and gritted his teeth, attempting to force the pain to the back of his mind.

Guiding Carly to the side door, he climbed in behind her and fell backward into the cold steel wall. Pulling his right leg into his chest, he massaged his ankle and watched out the six-inch by twelve-inch window.

Ethan had already sent Ben off. The kid ran back toward the building, drawing the crowd away from the blue pickup as he waved his hands in the air. Sprinting across the snow-dusted rear lot, Ben was able to lose most of those who followed as he weaved through the sparsely populated vehicles.

Reaching the pickup, Ethan waved the driver and his passenger out. "Let's go, we've got another vehicle. We can get you out—"

Before he could finish, the driver opened the door and stepped out. The thirty-something, dark haired gentleman stood nearly as tall as Ethan and had a good ten pounds on him. He looked back into the cab and then waved Ethan over. "My friend is hurt, she needs to see a doctor. I've got to get her inside. It can't wait."

As two wayward Feeders stepped away from the herd, Ethan pulled his baton and flicked it to full extension. "Stay here." Walking across the short greenbelt, he moved to the first and swung hard. The deep thud of solid steel striking bone was unmistakable as the body dropped. Dodging left, he swung backhand and winced as his shoulder reminded him of the events earlier in the day.

The second attacker failed to go down, and as Ethan wound back for another strike, an explosion from just beyond his line of sight, blew off the right half of the attacker's face. Following through, Ethan's lateral momentum carried him off his feet, and into the damp grass. Quickly rebounding, he stood and moved to the man holding the gun. "Thanks, but I'm sorry, I've got to cut this short. We really have to go. And listen, there's no one left in that hospital. They're all gone. You either come with us now or you're on your own. We've got plenty of room and the woman you just saw hop into that armored truck is a nurse. She may be able to help your friend. But it has to be now."

The man from the blue pickup glanced into the cab of the truck and back to Ethan. "Okay, let me get her out."

Ethan had already begun jogging back to the truck

as Ben reached the end of the employee parking lot. The kid jumped a six-foot wrought iron fence as if he we're stepping up onto a sidewalk, and was already sprinting back toward the building when Ethan called out. "Ben, let's go."

Reaching the truck, Ethan opened the side door and waited for Ben to climb inside. David and Carly sat with their backs to the cab, speaking in hushed tones as Ethan motioned out into the lot. "Those people from the blue pickup—they're coming with us. The passenger is hurt and needs some help."

Carly nodded and then got to her feet and stood at the door. "Okay, help them get inside and let's go."

Ethan moved to the pair now approaching and helped the woman passenger up into the truck. As the driver also stepped inside, Ethan paused at the door. *Where the hell am I going to take these people?*

Closing the door, Ethan moved into the driver's seat and started the armored vehicle. As Carly and David were getting familiar with the two new guests, Ben slipped down into the passenger's seat. Avoiding conversation, Ethan drove out through the exit at the opposite end of the parking lot.

Pulling out onto Longview Road, David knelt between the two front seats. "Ethan, what's the plan?"

"We need to find Shannon and then I'm going to my apartment. I need to get ahold of Emma and make sure she's okay. Then I'm going into the city— to get my mom and dad."

"Well then," David said. "You're gonna want to

hear what Carly has to say."

"David, nothing is going to change my mind, I'm—"

"She knows where Shannon is."

37

Left on Mineral Street, right on Fourth, and then the long winding maze to the backside of Ethan's building. Circling the block three times and pulling back into the alley, they'd found a small corner of their defeated city, free of those things—if only for the moment.

With the passenger side up against the rear wall of the building, and tucked nicely between two county dumpsters, the truck was nearly invisible to the cross-street thirty yards ahead. The sky had stopped dumping snow over an hour earlier and with the sun on its way toward the horizon, the shadows afforded by their current location all but guaranteed the group a few minutes of peace.

Draping a towel over the windshield and moving to the driver's door, Ethan and Ben slipped out into the alley. They ran through the courtyard, paused at the rear entrance, and with only two Feeders between them and the stairs, decided to make their move. Staying along the opposite wall and without being noticed, they slipped into the partially lit stairwell.

Again in possession of his weapon, Ethan led the way with the kid less than a step behind. Climbing the stairs two at a time, they reached his floor unfettered and with their confidence rising, they stepped out into the hall.

His apartment was twenty-five feet away. Between the door he'd just exited and where he needed to be, his former neighbor stood disemboweled. "Phil?" As the sixty-year-old retired plumber started in their direction, he stepped down on what was left of his large intestine. It dragged on the floor, leaving a trail of red from where another body lay facedown at the end of the hall.

With each step forward, more of what was left of his stomach ran out from beneath his red and black checkered flannel. As he moved to within ten feet, he stumbled forward, sending what remained from his midsection out onto the commercial grade carpeting.

Turning away, Ben shook his head. "You or me?"

"Watch the stairs; I'll get this one." Ethan moved to the opposite wall and took down the former plumber with one quick strike to the head. Retracting his baton, he moved into his apartment and closed the door. Into his bedroom, his cell phone still rested where he'd left it all those hours before. Atop his comforter it rested two feet from the charger that sat alone on the antique nightstand. "*I literally just need one thing to go my way today, just one.*"

Sliding his phone and charger into separate pockets, he moved into the bathroom. Stepping over a small mound of damp towels, he emptied what little remained in his medicine cabinet into a plastic bag. Back to the front door, he checked the peephole, and eyeing the fish-eyed hallway only spied Ben, waiting alone at the door to the stairs.

His weapon holstered and Ben carrying David's nine millimeter, they moved into the stairwell. Standing just inside the door, they paused and listened for any new threats. Silence, except for the moaning of the wood, concrete, and brick, as it expanded and settled with the warming temperatures of the midafternoon sun.

"Let's go." Quickly descending the stairs, they moved back into the lobby, again avoiding detection and then out through the rear doors and into the courtyard. Another twenty seconds and they were back at the truck, Ben through the driver's door first, followed closely by Ethan.

Plugging his phone into the makeshift charging station inside the glovebox, Ethan slumped down into the driver's seat, and finally took a breath. Six minutes and eleven seconds round-trip, and only one confrontation, Ethan counted this as his first victory of the day—aside from still having a heartbeat.

.   .   .

The group sat in the rear of the truck with their backs against the wall, attempting to make sense of what their world had become. Carly finished dressing Cora's side, as David made the long overdue introductions. "Ethan, this is Griffin. His friend here, the one with the hole in her hip, guzzling the water, is Cora."

Griffin looked around the cabin. "Thank you, all of you. We appreciate—"

Interrupting, Ethan turned to Carly, his heart rate just now returning to normal. "Where's Shannon?"

"Ethan, you need to understand the information I have was from earlier this morning. She may not even be—"

"I don't care. I'm going to get her, where is she?"

"The call came across the scanner just after nine o'clock this morning. Police dispatch said that she and a few others were trapped inside the bank."

"Then that's where we're going."

Moving back into the cab, Ethan slipped in behind the wheel. "Okay, I'm taking Main to Third. Anyone think that's a bad idea?"

No one spoke.

Ethan slowly rolled the armored truck forward, pushing the first dumpster far enough ahead so he could pull out into the alley. Driving along Main, he stayed in the center of the road and crept into each intersection. The streets in this part of town were virtually vacant, but for the many motionless corpses littering the sidewalks. It would appear his choice to come at the bank from the south was going to pay off. That was until he turned left onto Old Bridge Road.

Pulling to a stop at the corner of Old Bridge Road and Third Street, there was little doubt that the brick building sixty feet away was where he needed to be. More than twice the number of Feeders he'd run across at the hospital gathered at the entrance to First City Bank. They had yet to breach the perimeter, but with the crowd growing with each passing second, it was only a matter of minutes.

"Ethan, this is crazy," Carly said. "There is no way you're going to get past them."

"You wanna bet?"

"You don't even know if she's still in there. Shannon could have gotten out hours ago; it's not worth the risk."

"I'm not asking for permission. I'm also not asking that any of you to help. I know the risk, but I'm not leaving without finding her. She may not be in there, but I won't know if I don't try."

David leaned in and, wiping a thick layer of sweat from his face, said, "If you're going, I'm going. You're gonna need some backup."

"No," Ethan said. "I'm in and out in two minutes. Anyway, you're too old and with that ankle—you'll just slow me down."

His face a faint shade of pink, David stood and moved to the window. "We're the same age you smartass, and my ankle is fine."

Looking around the rear cabin, Carly shook her head. "I don't think this is a good idea. Even if she is in there. Trying to get through that mess is suicide. Can't we just wait them out?"

"Ethan, what's the plan?" David asked. "There's no way we'll make it through without—"

"Ben can you drive this thing?"

"Sure."

"Okay," Ethan said. "You drive along the sidewalk and take out as many as you can. The rest will follow you away from the building. Once they do, I'm going in. Take Old Bridge Road all the way down to Second and then double back through the alley. Make sure to drive slow enough that they don't lose interest and come back. Give me at least five minutes inside and then come back for me."

"Come back for us," Griffin said. "I figure now is as good a time as any to repay the favor."

"Alright, Griffin and I go in. We move fast. We get in, we get out, and then we get the hell out of here."

"I'm coming," David said. "You can't ask me not to; I've got more training than anyone in this truck."

Under his breath, Ethan laughed. "You look like crap, my friend, but you're right. Stay close and do not slow us down. I can only carry one person out of that building, and you know after last night, I may not even be up for that."

"You worry about you, I'll be fine."

38

The crowds outside First City Bank had grown in the time it took to run through the plan a second time. With the others only partially convinced of the merits of this endeavor, Ethan sat in the passenger seat with Ben behind the wheel of the armored truck. "Again, take your time leading them away. If you get into trouble or can't make it back, get to the end of Old Bridge Road and wait there. This rig is pretty much impenetrable. You guys will be safe."

"Okay," Ben said. "And Ethan, I'm sorry about earlier. I was just a little excited and knew with the gun I'd be able to draw them further away."

"I'll tell you what—you help me pull this off, and maybe we'll call it even."

. . .

Griffin knelt next to Cora as they backed onto the sidewalk, fifty feet from the bank. "You feeling any better?"

"Yeah, my stomach feels better. Carly said it had more to do with being out in the cold so long rather than my side. My head still hurts a little, but I'm pretty much good to go, and you?"

"Still cold, but I'm assuming the next few minutes will take care of that. Trying to avoid being eaten has a way of keeping you warm."

"Just make sure you get back here."

"Ten-four."

. . .

Stopped with the driver's door alongside the busted out front windows of Jennifer's Antiques, the armored vehicle's side mirror was less than six inches from the transparent jagged edges. Through the bulletproof windshield, the group watched as the crowd beyond began to take notice. A few peeled off and started in their direction as the men prepared to exit.

Carly stood at the rear door with one hand on David's forehead. "You're burning up. You shouldn't be going out there. I'm not trying to tell you what to do but—"

"I'm fine. It's just the booze from last night finally working its way out, or maybe I'm coming down with something. Either way, when I get back, I'll have the best nurse in the entire county to take care of me."

Carly frowned. She never frowned. "I don't like this, not at all. But I do love you, so get your butt back here, so I can show you how much."

David leaned in, and whispered, "Carly, you are the most wonderful person I have ever met. I can't imagine what my life would have been like, if I'd never taken that dare in fourth grade. Even more, I can't believe you actually let me kiss you. Given the chance, I'd still kiss you. Every. Single. Day. And yes, I've loved you ever since I was nine years old."

A tear rolled down her right cheek and slowed at the cleft in her chin. She leaned in and kissed him hard. "David, that was nearly as good as the day you proposed—where'd that come from?"

From the cab, Ethan barked, "Thirty seconds, then we go."

"What's gotten into him?" Carly asked.

David smiled. "Looks like that guy we lost in high school is back. Something changed in him at the hospital. I don't know what, but I think it's a good thing."

Stepping out from the passenger's seat, Ethan moved through the rear cabin. He motioned for Griffin to follow and then turned to Carly. "Lock the door behind us and don't open it again until you see our faces come out of that bank."

She told Ethan she understood, wished him luck, and then turned back to David. "Are you sure about this?"

He kissed her once again, as a tear matching hers hung at the corner of his right eye. "It's just something I have to do. There isn't any other way. I love you."

"Ben!" Ethan shouted. "Just like we talked about, sweep them away from the front, and then nice and slow. Clear the way, buddy." From the front seat, Ben gave the thumbs up.

The space outside the rear of the truck was clear.

Ethan opened the door and stepped out first. He was followed closely by David and then Griffin. Closing the door, the trio stayed in the shadow of the truck as it pulled away, gaining speed as it skipped over the next sidewalk and clipped the first few Feeders.

"Wait," Ethan said, his hand on David's shoulder. "Once the front doors are clear, we go. Fire on them only if we have to; I don't wanna draw any attention away from the truck."

To their left, inside the ravaged antique store, a four shelf mahogany cabinet slowly drifted away from the wall. Two rows of fine china sat above a shelf of porcelain baby figurines, and along the bottom, six stained-glass decanters. The one-hundred-year-old cabinet lurched up onto its front legs and pitched forward as a pair of curious Feeders moved away from their current victim.

Before the first piece of delicate glassware crashed to the stained concrete floor, Ethan stepped inside. With his sidearm placed securely on his right hip, he again drew the expandable steel baton. As the cabinet slammed to the floor, he stepped on top and kicked his first aggressor in the chest. Cartwheeling backward, the beast staggered into a vintage clothes rack and disappeared.

Coming in from behind, Griffin ran through as if he was on fire. Moving past Ethan before he could blink, the newest member of the group carried a stainless steel globe, slightly larger than a regulation size basketball. He gripped it by the stand and was already in mid-swing as he stepped by Ethan.

The area of the sphere labeled "*East Asia*" contacted the bridge of the Feeder's nose with a shallow crack, and both Griffin and Ethan turned away. Following through, fragmented pieces of bone and decomposed flesh exploded up and away as the Feeder dropped to the floor.

Not waiting for the first attacker to get back on its feet, Ethan grabbed Griffin by the shoulder and motioned back out to the sidewalk. "Let's go."

Stepping around the sea of broken glass, the trio moved quickly and quietly to the northeast corner of the building. Watching the armored vehicle slowly plow into the crowd, they stepped out onto the sidewalk and walked toward the entrance.

"Stay close," Ethan said.

Continuing along the sidewalk, the truck listed left as it pushed through the crowd, sideswiping the brick exterior. Gaining speed, the impenetrable fortress on wheels drifted along with its tires straddling the red painted curb. And as Ben cut the wheel hard to the right, the trailing edge of the truck pushed a half dozen Feeders in through the massive front windows of First City Bank.

Already in a dead sprint, Ethan flicked open the baton as he rushed toward the massive horde. Scanning the crowd, who had yet to take notice of his presence, he counted eleven that would be a direct threat and estimated there to be sixty or more who followed the truck off the sidewalk and up Old Bridge Road.

Twenty feet from the bank's entrance, Ethan

sensed that there was a problem. No one was at his side and peering down at the sidewalk, his shadow ran alone. Turning, he saw Griffin helping David up off the sidewalk. Back on their feet, the pair moved slowly, as David limp-walked toward Ethan.

Waving Ethan over, Griffin's mouth moved, but his voice was lost to the truck's overbearing engine. Attempting to assist the injured man, Griffin was hastily brushed off. And as Ethan took his first step back toward his best friend, David fell face-first onto the unforgiving concrete.

39

Moving quickly back to his friend, Ethan motioned toward the massive opening at the front of the bank. "Griffin, I'll get him inside. Just get in there before we do and make sure there aren't any surprises."

Again on his feet, David clung to Ethan's vest. Being dragged, the two-hundred pound man began vomiting blood. As the Feeders who were thrown into the bank emerged, he begged Ethan to leave him. "Go find Shannon, we all aren't going to make it. Please, do it for me, do it for Carly. I'm begging you, I can't go back to her."

Reaching the partially demolished entrance to the bank and watching the truck disappear behind the ocean of bodies, Ethan pushed David inside, over to the wall, and held his shoulders pinned back. "I don't know what you're doing, but it's gotta wait. Do you think you could do me a favor and stay alive for another few minutes?"

"It doesn't look like I have a choice."

The bank had obviously been overrun at some point earlier in the day, Ethan was sure of it. Desks were overturned, light fixtures smashed, and computer monitors lay facedown among the mess of Savings Account and Home Equity handouts. The most telling sign—the door between the bank's lobby and the secured teller area had been torn from its hinges.

Rapid footfalls came from out of the darkened interior and then Griffin appeared. He stood beside Ethan and motioned toward the rear of the bank. "Hey, there are voices coming from the vault. Maybe it's the woman you're looking for?"

David spoke, although his voice drifted off as quickly as it had come. "You can actually hear—"

"Ethan," Griffin said, "what the hell is the matter with him?"

David was sick. Not unlike the flu that kept him out of school for the entire week of finals his senior year, but still different. His hands shook. He was just barely upright. The skin on his face and neck had gone from a light shade of pale to nearly translucent. His deep blue eyes were beginning to cloud over. And then there was the thick trail of vomit-blood running from the right corner of his mouth, yeah he was sick. Perfect timing.

"Flu, maybe—I don't know? But, we really don't have time for this... look." Ethan pointed out into the street. The majority of the crowd continued to follow the truck away from the building, but not all of them took the bait. At least twenty, give or take a few, found the activity back at the bank more interesting than following the moving metal box on wheels, or maybe they were just lazy. Either way, going back out into the street wasn't going to be an option.

"Griffin," Ethan said. "You see any of those things in the back near the vault?"

"No, just the voices, I think. Either way, whoever's back there is safe for now."

"Okay, we're gonna need to stay out of sight for few minutes as well. Hopefully it will give the ones out in the street time to lose interest and move on."

Stepping away from the wall, David straightened up. He no longer walked with a limp, and started for the rear of the bank. Past the Branch Manager's office, around the downed security door, and in between the teller's desks, he squinted into the darkness, trying to get a clear image of his surroundings. Finding a place to sit, he flopped down into a rolling desk chair and began to cough.

Finished with their scan of the interior, and without another way out of the bank, Ethan and Griffin moved in behind the teller's counter and knelt alongside their sick friend. After wiping the sweat away from David's face and what remained along his friend's mouth and chin, Ethan sat in silence, listening for the voices Griffin had described.

Nothing for a full two minutes, and with the lobby beginning to fill with Feeders, Ethan slid out from under the counter. Crouching, he pushed the chair and his friend into the hall and motioned for Griffin to follow. Ten feet from the vault door he said, "I'm going in."

He didn't wait for either man to question his plan

or even respond. Ethan turned and crawled away from the counter. Rising, he moved to the opposite end of the hall and stood in the shadow of the massive vault door. Reaching for the inch-thick stainless-steel handle, he slowly pulled it open.

As light spilled out into the hall, Ethan stepped around the door. Not what he expected to find, the empty room held little more than the two hundred safety deposit boxes and a granite topped table in the back left corner. The voices, he'd heard them as well, but not from here.

"Ethan."

He'd asked Griffin to keep all communication to a minimum, but as he moved back into the hall, he could see why his request had been ignored. Fifteen feet away, on all fours, his best friend crawled toward the vault. Slowly progressing out of the dark, David was closely pursued by two Feeders, and then Griffin, who was in the process of leveling his weapon at their attackers.

One quick shot to the head sent the first beast into the second, and then both stumbled forward into David. Coming from behind, Griffin struggled to make sense of the three bodies as David began to shout. "Leave me—just go."

Starting back toward his friend, something over Ethan's right shoulder stirred. A door opened and another source of light reached out and connected with what slipped from the vault. As Griffin moved in, stomped the second Feeder, and pulled David free, Ethan turned back toward the opening door.

Rick Norcross, the bank's morning teller, emerged from the sparsely stocked supply room. Four years Ethan's senior, the overweight, balding, father of two was followed out into the partially lit hall by Amy Hildebrandt. The newest assistant manager of First City Bank was a transfer out of the city and had only received her new business cards three days before.

Shouting incoherently as they ran, Rick appeared to not notice the others as he moved into the vault, and as Amy followed the older man inside, she begged Ethan to follow. As the two bank employees moved by, one last shadow emerged from the supply room.

As she did every other day, the woman running toward Ethan wore a red blouse and jet-black polyester slacks. She moved quickly in only her socks, and cried as her eyes fell upon the man she'd worked with for the last six months. "Ethan, thank God."

Since his first day of employment with BXF, the closest contact he'd had with the distant blonde was handing her a manila envelope that had slipped from her overly-organized desk. He'd often wondered what it would feel like to wrap her five-foot four-inch frame in his arms. And as she leapt into his embrace, it felt different than he imagined. Amazing, but still not exactly what he had expected.

"Shannon, you're okay. I'm getting you out of here." Ethan didn't know if this was true—he didn't know anything, but that was the only thing on his mind.

Letting her go, Ethan watched as another six Feeders rounded the corner and started toward the vault. At the same time, Griffin had David back on his feet moving slightly ahead of the crowd. As they passed Ethan and turned into the vault behind Shannon, David tripped over the entrance and slid into the bottom row of safety deposit boxes on the right hand wall.

Ethan stood at the door and fired four rounds into the crowd as another three turned the corner. "Guys, I think—"

Griffin stepped to the threshold and grabbed Ethan by the shoulder. "Let's go, we don't have the firepower for this. Get in here."

Reluctantly stepping back and into the vault, Ethan quickly holstered his weapon and moved to David. Sliding his friend up and into a seated positon, he began searching him for injuries from the last attack. David pushed him away and spit a mouthful of blood out onto the floor.

Slightly less coherent than he was out on the sidewalk, David lay with his back against the wall. Turning to the left, he attempted to reach out for Griffin as the door descended into its closed position. Next the sound of metal on metal as the twenty-ton door found its seal.

As Griffin stood to the right of the door, he scanned the interior control pad. Without knowing what he was looking for, he turned to the others who'd taken to consoling one another and said, "How do we lock this thing?"

No one answered. No one even looked up.

Turning back to the control pad, Griffin stared at the six rows of alpha-numeric keys and finally located the green *Auto-Lock* button. Before Amy, the newest assistant branch manager could stop him, Griffin pressed the button.

40

Thirty minutes had passed since they found themselves locked in the three-hundred-fifty square foot, custom made vault. The air had grown stale and although the power had been out for the last few hours, the backup generators continued to function, keeping the space at an even seventy-two degrees.

The group of six sat with their backs against the wall and detailed their individual stories of where they'd been and what they'd done before ending up at this point. The specific events were different for each person, but the theme remained the same across all six stories. Simply survive. Run, hide, fight, do whatever you have to do to survive. This was their new reality.

Ethan now sat with David, who continued to fade in and out of consciousness. With the others occupied at the control pad, he again watched his friend come back. "Ethan, you have to get out."

"David, you're sick buddy. You're not thinking straight. We're gonna get you out of here and get you some help."

His voice now clear and increasing the volume,

David said, "I'm not sick, Ethan."

"You're definitely sick my man, maybe the flu. And it looks like the fever has you a little confused."

Pushing away from his friend, David slid into the corner. Reaching down, he pulled his right sleeve up into his armpit, revealing two separate wounds. Swallowing hard, he looked into Ethan's eyes. "I'm not sick and there is no getting better. This is it for me."

Griffin turned away from the others and stared at Ethan. "He's bitten? When the hell were you going to let the rest of know?"

Ethan didn't respond. He continued to look back at David and shook his head. "This can't be. You never... I mean you didn't even... when did this—"

David took a deep breath as the others moved away from the control pad and stood with their backs against the rear wall of safety deposit boxes. "In the hospital, when I fell into those tables, just before you came over. I was trying to pull my fat ass out of there, and didn't notice one of those things was behind the glass case. He got ahold of my arm and there wasn't much I could do. You should have just let me end it there."

"Why didn't you say anything?" Ethan asked. "Why'd you let us keep—"

"I needed to make sure Carly was safe. It's as simple as that. And now I need you to keep your promise."

"What?"

"Ethan, don't make me say the words. You know

253

what needs to be done here. Carly can never see me like that. I wanted to do it myself and you took that opportunity away from me. Now you have to do it. And get these people out of this room before it happens."

"Uh, we may have a problem." Amy moved back over to the control pad. "We aren't getting out of here anytime soon."

"Excuse me?" Ethan said.

"You see, when the vault door is locked from the inside, the only one who has the code to open it is the manager. And well, he's obviously not here. That's the way your boss had this thing built. He's a bit of a control freak, only two people have the code to open it once it's closed. Silvio Marquez and one other person."

"Who's that?"

"Your sister, Emma."

"That's it then, we all just die in here?"

"No," Amy said. "The door is also set to reopen every weekday at ten after five. That corresponds with the end of your route and happens regardless of who's managing the bank. So, at five-ten that door is going to swing open automatically. Whoever or whatever is still out there is going to be let in. Let's just pray that those things get bored and walk away within the next two hours."

Griffin stepped forward, his hand outstretched. He held a five-foot section of audio cable that was sitting just inside the door to the vault when he entered. "Ethan, I don't think he has two hours. I'm sorry, but we need to do something right now to make sure that the rest of us aren't in any danger."

Sitting forward, David began to cough, but quickly recovered. "He's right. I don't have two hours. I know this. The pain in my arm is gone. So is the headache and the nausea. I can't feel my legs and your faces are all blurred. It's mostly just shadows and sound at this point."

Closing his eyes, David continued. "There's thing one you need know to me for it."

Griffin looked around the room and said to Ethan, "He's not making any sense, he's delirious. We need to tie him up. Those people we ran across on the mountain, they were turning in a matter of minutes."

Nodding, Ethan grabbed the audio cable from Griffin and moved to David. "I'll do it."

Griffin stepped back and watched as Ethan looped the cable tightly around David's wrists. "Ethan, what do we do if—I mean you've got to—"

Finished securing the thick cable around his friend's wrist, Ethan finally spoke. "Yes, you're right, but I don't know that I'm ready to end my friend's life just yet."

"Ethan," Shannon said. "It looks like he's already gone."

"She's right," Griffin said. "You'll be doing him a favor and making sure that the rest of us—"

"Wait." David was awake, if only for the moment. "There's something you need to hear."

The others looked to Ethan as he stepped forward.

"David, please."

"Ethan I'm..." His words trailed off as he lurched forward and arched his back. Blood ran from his left ear and he quickly slid into a heap on the concrete floor.

Moving in next to David, Ethan dropped his head against his friend's chest. The room went silent as he listened. Thirty seconds turned into sixty, which turned into five minutes. Nothing. Slowly pulling away, he brought his friend's eyelids down and stood. "No one touches him. You all understand?"

"Do it! You know what's happening to him, just do it. You're putting everyone at risk." Griffin now saying what everyone was thinking.

Ethan didn't respond.

"Give me the gun, I'll do it." Griffin wasn't backing down. Since entering the vault behind the two bank employees and pulling the door shut, he had yet to let up.

Ethan turned to Griffin as the others stepped back. "Last time, keep quiet! You're the reason we're stuck in here. I'm not going to ask you again."

"Oh yeah I forgot, you're the big shot with the uniform and the badge. So tell me, what's your plan—huh?"

Ethan began to answer, but was cut short. "You do realize that I just followed you and the others in here. And with those—those things outside the door, you're all real lucky I even thought to shut it behind us. If I hadn't, you'd all be dead or worse," Griffin pointed at David. "You'd be just like him."

Turning away, he again focused on his friend. Sliding the pistol to David's forehead, he dropped to one knee, grabbed the back of his head, and pulled him in tight. "You don't deserve this. It should have been me." Ethan leaned in and placed his mouth just outside his friend's bloodstained ear. "I will get to Carly. I will get her somewhere safe. I promise you that."

His friend's body began to go rigid. Ethan felt the beast that was David beginning to struggle. Leaning away and starting to stand, what little remained of his friend was now and forever gone. The wounds along his right triceps oozed a yellowish-orange fluid that leaked out into the pool of coagulated blood surrounding their feet.

Peering into David's eyes, they were unrecognizable as human. The remaining fragments of his friend were quickly losing the battle with what had taken hold. Beginning to growl, the beast now moving slowly toward Ethan wore his friend's face, but was not him. Pulling at his restraints, the animal that David had become fought to free itself as the group all took a step back.

Twisting against the audio cable, his left arm gave way and the resulting sound of snapping bone reverberated through the cramped vault. The realization that David had just broken his own arm in an attempt to free himself hung in the air, but what appeared to put an exclamation on the moment was the fact that his friend hadn't even flinched. He didn't look at the injury and only stared across the room at the five unbelieving individuals.

Turning from the others and again raising his weapon, Ethan heard their gasps only just before he realized his friend was loose. David shot forward as if out of a cannon. He slammed headfirst into Ethan's chest, sending both men to the blood-soaked concrete floor and the nine millimeter pistol drifting into the corner.

Shielding himself from David's snapping jaws, Ethan pulled back his legs and kicked straight up. He drove his friend's body back into the row of safety deposit boxes and twisted right in hopes of finding the weapon he'd just dropped. No luck, the only thing in his inverted field of view were the four others, now scrambling to either side.

As Ethan moved up and onto his knees, scanning the vault for his weapon, David shot forward again. Turning away, Ethan held out his right hand, trying to deflect the initial blow. He anticipated a direct hit and assumed that following the collision, he'd again be flat on his back. He pictured being torn apart without even the most remote chance of defending himself. This is where he figured his life would end.

Clenching his jaw, he twisted right as David lunged forward. Their bodies slammed into one another like two bags of wet sand, sending Ethan back and into the bottom row of safety deposit boxes, his head making contact first. Blinking through the pain, he attempted to take a deep breath, but failed. This was it, the end.

As his friend climbed on top and moved his way

up toward Ethan's face, his vision began to fade. Next, the low hum in his ears indicated that unconsciousness was close. If he had any hope of walking out of this bank alive, he needed to do something now. Only there was a problem. His arms were pinned down to the floor below.

With David now upright and his arms free, Ethan was only able to get glimpses of the battle he was losing. In between the shouts and screams, his mind waded in the shadows until it finally decided to give up. The last image to flash through his narrowed field was the nine millimeter he'd held to his friend's head only moments before, and the glint of the barrel.

41

6:00 PM...

He couldn't quite place his surroundings. It was dark and his feet were heavy, the wind on his face much cooler than he remembered. There was a brilliant pain at the top of his head, a constant pounding that radiated down into the base of his skull and between his shoulders. He sensed that he was being dragged, his boots skipping off the asphalt and moving toward a pair of glowing beacons somewhere off in the distance.

"Ethan, were going home."

The voice was crystal clear, but he had yet to recognize its owner. Attempting to speak, he only managed a few words. "Where is my friend?"

"Come on, Ethan, keep moving. We're almost there."

Another voice, this time speaking to the first. "Is she okay? What did you tell her?"

A woman... he knew this person, but not well. Her tone was familiar, but the memory still clouded.

Her voice again. "How'd they clear the streets?"

"That kid standing at the door—Ben, he's been driving up and down the block for hours. Those things finally all followed the truck away from the building."

As the lights ahead merged into one, Ethan closed his eyes and breathed in deep. The sting of spent fuel burned the back of his throat, and the idling engine brought him back to the present. "Where is he?"

There was no response.

Turning away from the glare of the armored vehicle's headlights, Ethan opened his eyes. He had one arm slung over Griffin and the other rested atop Shannon's shoulders. They dragged him to the rear of the truck and sat him on the extended rear bumper. "What's going on, where's David?"

As the words left his mouth, Carly had turned the corner and appeared from out of his field of vision. She sat next to him on the bumper, wrapped her arms around his neck, and pulled him in close. "Ethan, he's gone. David was bitten at the hospital and—" The moment took her. Carly began to sob heavily, thick tears running down her face and onto his shirt. "He attacked you."

She folded into him, the two held each other and cried like they'd never before. As the memories began to come back to Ethan, he wiped his wet face and looked up. Griffin and Shannon stood ten feet away in the shadow of the full moon. With their backs to the truck, they watched as the two bank employees strode to their vehicles and drove off.

Ethan kissed Carly on the forehead and asked her

if she would check on Ben and Cora. He knew if she felt like she was needed, her mind wouldn't have much time for anything else. As she walked to the side of the truck, Ethan turned back to Griffin and Shannon. "What the hell happened in there?"

Half expecting this, Griffin said, "You know what happened, you were there. Except for the difficult part, where you hesitated and left it up to us to clean up the mess."

"Mess?" Ethan said. "Putting a bullet into the head of someone I've known for my entire life, is that what you're referring to as my mess?"

"Listen," Griffin said, "You're still here because of us—so maybe a little gratitude wouldn't hurt."

"Who did it?"

"Who did what?"

"Who killed David?"

"He was dead before he walked into that bank, you know that."

"No," Ethan said. "Who took my gun and actually put a bullet in his head?"

Griffin looked directly into Ethan's eyes. "I did—there was no other way. You'd be dead right now if—"

Shannon looked at Griffin. She shook her head, turned, and walked back toward the truck.

"He was my friend," Ethan said. "My only friend, so excuse me if I don't thank you and shake your hand just yet."

As the truck continued to idle, Ben appeared at the side door. "Listen guys, we've got to go. The last wave we cleared out is headed back this way, and I didn't spend the last three hours clearing them for nothing. Let's go."

Griffin nodded. "Ethan, I understand. And I'm sorry, but I didn't have a choice. I hope that you can trust me on that."

"I'm trying to."

Griffin started for the side door and Ethan followed. They climbed into the rear cabin and moved in beside the others. Ethan's vision still a bit blurry, and the pounding in his head not yet subsiding, he took a seat against the wall as Griffin remained standing near the door.

All eyes turned to Carly as she used the sleeve of her uniform jacket to wipe away the tears and began to compose herself. "This thing... whatever it is, has the ability to wipe out all of us—every last human on this planet. The reason I say this *Thing*, is because no one yet knows what it is. When I got to work this morning, the emergency room was full and there were at least twenty deep waiting. To say that we were overwhelmed would be the understatement of the year."

As Ben pulled the armored truck out into the street, Ethan sat forward. "Those people from the Chili-fest?"

"Some," Carly said. "But also some locals too. Most were complaining of something happening out at John's farm when they were setting up. They said they were being attacked. We just figured the drunks from the night before were getting a bit rowdy. That was until the first one passed. Bed number three, the older gentleman stopped breathing and no one even knew. He was bitten in the back and because we were so busy, no one thought to go check on him."

Cora reached for Carly's hand. "He ended up like the others?"

"Yes, as one of the other nurses wheeled him out of the ER, he sat straight up and—"

"So," Griffin said, "it looks like these people that are bitten are infected somehow. Any ideas what could cause something like this?"

Shaking her head, Carly said, "It doesn't make sense. Nothing about it does. It's not viral, it's not bacterial, and it doesn't present as an antigen."

"How do you know?"

"Well this is the part that may make your skin crawl. After about the first hour, hospital administration contacted the CDC. We were told that they were already aware of the situation and that we may need to turn away anyone showing signs of infection. They said we should have a police presence at the entrance and take whatever precautions were necessary."

"What did they want you to do, just let people die?"

"They never really gave us specific instructions, but we found out later that they'd been dealing with this for almost a week. The scary part is that they still had no idea what it was."

"Had no idea?"

"After about ten this morning, they stopped

answering their phones, although we received a broadcast email shortly afterward that said we should take whatever measures were necessary to survive. They called this a Global Event."

Rubbing his temples, Ethan said, "What does that mean? For us, right here right now? Could this thing eventually just run its course?"

"We just don't know. The best thing we can do right now is to find others and get somewhere safe. Somewhere secluded maybe. But not here."

"Why not?"

"Have any of you heard of the Xavier Brevin Mental Health facility? The one about an hour north, just outside Thomasville?"

"The insane asylum?" Cora said.

"Well... yes. When all this happened earlier today, they were overrun and as the gates came down, all six-hundred criminally insane patients spilled out into the streets. Last we heard, they'd completely destroyed Thomasville and were headed here."

"So," Ethan said, "we leave. All of us, we drive out—"

Ben pulled into the shadows and parked the truck at the end of Old Bridge Road. He turned from the driver's seat and said, "Ethan, your phone has been blowing up. You have like a million messages."

"It's Emma... excuse me."

Ethan joined Ben in the cab and pulled his phone from the charger. Sixteen text messages and eight voicemails. All but one from his sister.

He scrolled first through his text messages, the

majority were simply Emma questioning his whereabouts. However, the last few described the same hell he and his friends were going through and that his sister was scared. She'd lost her job and someone named Richard Daniels was helping her.

Switching to his voicemail, it was much of the same. Before finishing the calls from his sister, he keyed up the only message that wasn't from her. His mother called and asked if he'd seen the news and said that she and his father were going to stay put. His dad hadn't been feeling well and getting in the car in his present condition, "*Wasn't something he wanted to do.*" She said that the streets near the house were a bit noisy and asked that he call her when he could.

Returning to the last voicemail from his sister, he pressed play.

42

Her voice was different. It was something he couldn't quite describe. Not anger, and not quite stress. Her words came quicker as if she was racing to get them all out at once. This was an Emma he'd yet to meet.

"Ethan, please. I need you to let me know somehow, that you're okay. I got a few weird texts from mom this morning and I think maybe her and dad need some help. I'm back in California now, so please let me know—"

The sound of brakes locking, and then the squeal of tires gripping the roadway. He pulled the phone away, looked at the display and then pressed it back to his ear.

The next sound, his sister taking a deep breath.

Twenty seconds of nothing and then she was back, but not speaking into the phone. *"Bret... Chad?"*

Not another voice.

The familiar sound of shattering glass and then a distant growl.

Turning into the rear cabin, every eye rested on

him. The group of five collectively held their breath as Ethan stared down at his phone.

"I'm going to California—to find my sister."

WHAT'S NEXT?
Book Two – *DEVASTATION*

Turn the page for a look inside the next book in
The Last Outbreak Series.

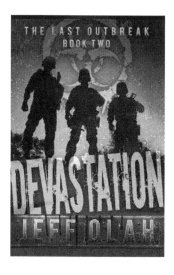

Also, be among the first to get notified about Jeff
Olah's new releases.
Join the mailing list at: JeffOlah.com/Newsletter

Excerpt from Book Two
DEVASTATION

Prologue

Twelve Months before the Outbreak...

She was going to be fired and thrown out of the building at some point today, of this she was almost certain.

Staring back at the video she'd watched more than a dozen times, Shannon Briggs had a decision to make. She had two options; however, she already knew how the next hour was going to play out. And the scorching pain in the pit of her stomach told her that what she was about to do was unquestionably the right thing.

Out of the corner of her eye, Shannon watched as the last few seconds ticked away. Reaching her phone, she turned down the reminder, switched it to vibrate, and slipped it into her coat pocket. Before standing, she moved back to her desktop, saved her work, and waited as the flash drive recorded her last session.

With the video paused in the upper right corner of her monitor, Shannon rolled it back to the twenty second mark and made a mental note of each of the four men occupying the screen. The small man running in from the left, the overweight gentleman in the lab coat, the third man gripping the pistol, and the body beginning to rise from the floor.

Taking a screen capture, Shannon dragged the image to the printer icon and stared back at the screen as the vivid colors poured out onto the stock white eight and a half by eleven. While the printer finished its task, she closed the video playback program and powered off her machine.

"Okay, I guess it's now or never."

Peering through the doorway and out into the hall, her hand shook as she reached into the top drawer of her desk and removed her keys. One of only two personal items remaining at the office after taking her external hard drive home the night before. Shannon slid them into her coat pocket and started for the elevator.

Out into the connecting hall, she paused before entering the elevator bay. Intently focused on the men's faces adorning the graphic image, she missed the doors opening and closing two separate times. As the bell signaling her third opportunity sounded, the doors parted only seconds before his voice poured out. "Ms. Briggs, you joining us this morning?"

Starting toward the elevator car ten feet away, she slipped the photo into her bag and looked up. "Mr. Goodwin, I... I was just finishing up with—"

"Don't do that, don't ever do that."

Marcus Goodwin. Deep set blue eyes. Clean shaven. Chiseled jawline. Six feet tall and one hundred eighty pounds of pure intimidation. He wore the exact same black power suit and navy blue tie every single day, today it was pin striped. Black imported Italian leather loafers and charcoal grey embroidered socks completed his persona. He hated small talk and despised incompetence.

Stepping into the glass-lined car, Shannon didn't make eye contact, although it wouldn't have mattered. The man standing only inches away peered down at his phone and quickly scrolled through a wall of text as he continued. "Don't explain yourself. Don't try to be what I want you to be. Just do your job."

"Yes, I understand—"

"Do you?"

"Yes."

"Good, because you're going to get the opportunity to prove it. Our guests arrived thirty minutes early and I've had them taken to the Nevada conference room. I've been monitoring them from my office and have a good idea that this may not go well. Mr. Daniels isn't going to want to hear what I have to tell him, and may look to you for confirmation."

"I'm aware of why they're here."

"Ms. Briggs, do you know why I brought you here over seven years ago? I hired you specifically for this project and for your special talent. I expect that you will see to it that everyone in that room walks away with an absolute sense of confidence in what BXF Technologies is doing, as well as a big fat smile."

She didn't answer. Shannon simply nodded and in looking back upon her own reflection, straightened her coat. As Marcus Goodwin turned back to his phone and with a slight grin beginning to form at the corner of his mouth, she took a slow breath in through her nose and dropped her hands to her side.

The bell rang signaling they'd reached the first floor and as the doors began to part, Shannon instinctively leaned forward. However, before she raised her right foot from the Italian marble, Goodwin cut his eyes at her. Without turning his head, he paused for a moment, waited for her to straighten up, and then started out into the hall ahead of her. He stepped hard. Each footfall pounding like an exclamation point.

Waiting for him to move out of sight, Shannon stared at the floor and shook her head. Speaking only to herself as new passengers paused at the door, she said, "What a gentleman."

Out into the hall, she strode quickly to match Goodwin's pace. And by the time they reached the intersecting corridor, she was on his heels. Turning into the lobby, he marched to the front counter and approached the four receptionists behind the mahogany and glass enclosure. To the thin, dark-haired woman still on a call, he leaned over the counter and motioned toward the opposite end of the room. "Our guests... do they have everything I requested?"

Ripping off her headset, her hand shook as she placed the call on hold. "Yes, Mr. Goodwin, everything was in place before they entered the conference room, but..."

"But what—is there a problem?"

"No, it's just that Mr. Daniels has come out here quite a few times. He wanted to know what was taking—"

"He seemed impatient," Goodwin said, his tone coming off more like a statement than a question.

"Yes."

"What did you tell him?"

"I told them that you were extremely busy and would arrive at the scheduled meeting time."

"This made him angry?"

"I think so. He didn't say anything. He just turned and walked back into the room."

"Good." Peering down at her name plate, he smiled. "Dolores Marquez, you did very well."

"Thank you, Mr. Goodwin, I appreciate—"

Turning away and looking around the open space, Goodwin interrupted. "Dolores, where is Michael from the IT group? He was supposed to be here five minutes ago."

She smiled. "He's already in the room. He said he

wanted to get everything ready for you and Ms. Briggs."

As Goodwin slammed his fist onto the counter, Dolores rocked back in her chair. "I'm sorry, Mr. Goodwin. I didn't know that—"

"He's in the room now?"

The small woman appeared to fold into herself. "Yes, he hasn't come out since—"

Goodwin turned and started across the expansive lobby. Passing the gargantuan double doors that framed the entrance to the building, he briefly glanced back as Shannon struggled to keep pace. "Once we're finished here today, I'll need you to remind me to fire Michael."

She didn't meet his eyes and as he turned away, she quickly reached back into her coat. Pulling out her phone, Shannon powered it off and let it slide back in. She moved alongside Goodwin and couldn't look away as the back of his ears turned a raucous shade of red. She couldn't help but imagine a thick layer of steam would soon follow.

His speed increased with each new step and as they moved by the black leather sofas at the center of the lobby, Shannon looked toward the east wall. Just over seven years earlier, she'd walked through the doors at her back and sat nearly in this same location. And she waited exactly twenty-eight minutes for the privilege to be interviewed by Marcus Goodwin himself.

She remembered staring back at the same colossal water treatment covering the sixty foot wall she was now rushing toward, and the calm it brought. Spreading itself from the bank of elevators to the building's entrance, the deluge was surprisingly quiet. This morning, watching the backlit water slowly make its way down the uneven rock face, she begged for that calm to return.

The warm glow of orange and the underplayed yellows near the top of the stone wall bled into the soft, inviting blue mist near the black stone pool bordering its foundation. Breathing in through her nose brought the relaxing scent of chamomile and lavender. She assumed Goodwin intended this, even though she'd never asked. There wasn't anything placed inside this building without reason. He had a plan for every inch of the massive concrete and steel structure.

Within ten feet of the room, the combative voices had already begun to pour out into the hall. One in particular roared above the others and called for the man she now walked beside. Through the distorted mess of fluctuating voices, the only words she was able to make out were *Goodwin, fraud,* and *done*.

Reaching the conference room doors, Shannon assumed Goodwin had also heard the comments and as he stopped before the threshold, she turned and looked into his eyes. Expecting a reaction just short of apocalyptic, she only smiled and waited for him to respond.

"Ms. Briggs," a half smile resembling hers slid across his face. "Walk in first, sit down at the back of the room, and wait for me to give you the floor. If any of the men in this room ask you a question, comment on the weather, or even compliment your dress, you are to ignore them. I want you to act as if you and I are alone in that room."

He paused; however, she didn't respond and knew that if she waited, he'd continue.

And he did. "When I am done with Daniels, I will ask for your assessment. He will also want to hear what it is you have to say and will be looking for confirmation. At that point, you will address the room and when you are finished, I will have them escorted out of the building. I don't want this small bump in the road to turn into a three-ring circus. Let's tell them only what they need to hear and send them home."

She'd either have to stand with the man who was about to alter the course of human history or lie to their visitors. Neither of these options made her feel any better about walking into that room on the other side of the door. She could do the right thing and take whatever demented punishment Goodwin decided to hand down. And currently her need for self-preservation, as well as a steady paycheck, was winning the battle with her inner voice of reason.

"Let's go," he said holding the door open.

Shannon stepped to the left, waited as Goodwin pushed the door all the way open, and as the conversation inside dropped off, walked to the rear of the room. She moved to the last seat at the rear of the table and sat down. She didn't make eye contact with their guests and instead, stared straight into the sixty-inch screen at the opposite end of the massive conference table.

The three men occupying the room turned quickly toward the doorway. Marcus Goodwin stepped through and moved without hesitation to the man nearest the screen and extended his right arm. "Daniels, to what do we owe this surprise visit? I was under the assumption that you had your hands full at my facility in the mountains. This time of year it had to be quite a trek?"

As the men shook hands, Shannon marveled at their similarities. They wore roughly the same suit and striped blue ties, although neither seemed to notice. She knew Goodwin had just turned fifty-five, although the man he offered his hand to looked to be ten years his senior. Same dashing good looks, the kind you'd envy gracing the cover of a magazine, but with a softer edge. They were also nearly the same height and looked to be within ten pounds of one another. The two could have easily passed for siblings.

She was first introduced to Major Richard Daniels two years before and had been in his company more than a dozen times since then. On each occasion, she found him warm and inviting. She had yet to figure out if that was his way, or if he felt the same sense of mediocrity in Goodwin's presence. From where she currently stood, it looked like the former.

"Marcus, I didn't come all the way just for the

pleasure of your company and you know that." He shook Goodwin's hand and moved to the far side of the screen. "You need to understand something." He grabbed the remote from the conference room table, gazed at it for a second, and then handed it to the young man to his left. "Michael—can you rewind this thing? Back to the beginning, where the soldier goes to the ground?"

Goodwin leaned in and grabbed the remote before his young technician had the chance. "Michael doesn't work for you. He works for me—well he used to." Moving to the high back chair that sat across the table from a yet unidentified man taking notes, he continued. "Michael, I need you to go back to your department, drop off your badge, and then find your way to Human Resources. I will have someone meet you there in twenty minutes. Do not be late, I don't want to have to send someone out to look for you."

Confusion peppered the young man's face. "Mr. Goodwin?"

"Just go. I can handle anything these men need."

The young man with a flawless set of pearly whites, neatly trimmed jet-black hair, and unblemished olive-colored skin, hung his head. "I'm sorry." The corners of his mouth downturned, it was apparent that he had no idea why he was apologizing. He turned to the guests, grabbed his cell phone, and then walked out of the room.

Major Richard Daniels shook his head as he turned his attention away from the young man exiting the room and focused once again on

Goodwin. "You've got to be the most narcissistic man on the entire planet. You have no regard—"

"Yes, yes I know. I've heard that from you one too many times. Now let's get to the point of this little meeting."

"That's part of why we're here. Your ego is going to kill this project and by association, my men."

"Collateral damage," Goodwin said. "It happens. No one can make the world's best omelet without breaking a few eggs. And along the same vein, we aren't going to create the world's most adaptive soldier without a few sacrifices. It's just part of doing business."

Major Daniels had yet to acknowledge that Shannon was sitting less than fifteen feet away. He continued as he moved in near the man taking notes and sat across the table from Goodwin. "That's not the only problem."

Growing tired of the conversation but willing to listen for another moment, Goodwin sat back and folded his arms. "Yes?"

"We are testing this thing—"

"This thing?" Goodwin said interrupting.

"Excuse me," Major Daniels said. "We are currently testing the Ares injectable at more than two hundred locations. Early tests were promising, but it's time we slow this down and get a handle on why these incidents continue to occur."

Without making eye contact and as the last syllable left Daniels mouth, Goodwin barked, "No, we're moving ahead."

"You don't have the authority—"

"The site managers all report here," Goodwin said. "And they have instructions to continue with the tests."

"Watch the video, you may have a different opinion."

Rewinding the short clip, Goodwin said, "I've viewed it twice." Pushing the play button and as the shaky images flowed across the screen, he asked, "Is this why you're here?"

An overweight lab technician was the first to appear, followed closely by an armed guard. They both stood over a lifeless corpse whose upper torso, neck, and face had been torn apart by a yet unknown source.

A third much smaller man entered the frame, pointed down at the body and then peered into the camera. "Another one. He was attacked less than two minutes earlier and flatlined only seconds ago. This is the third—"

The small man was interrupted as the body began to push away from the floor and reached for his ankle. He pulled away and stepped aside as the man with the pistol moved in. The camera turned away as the deafening sound of the weapon being fired ended the short clip.

"I have six more of these to show you," Daniels said. "It has officially gone too far. We need someone else to oversee this project. We should have never let Lockwood leave. He was the only one who knew what this was and how to fix it."

"I've seen all the footage. It's just more of the same in a different location. And we needn't bother ourselves with that man—I've already got my eye on someone else. We have no need for Dr. Lockwood. His ideas didn't align with what we are trying to do here."

"We?" Daniels said. "I hate to burst that delusional little bubble you're living in, but you're the only one who believes this project is anything but a train wreck at this point. And I'm making the recommendation to our friends that we put this project on hold. I'm not going to let them put another dollar into this without some sort of oversight."

"I'll tell you what—you go ahead and make whatever recommendation you see fit. This is going to happen with or without you. And just so there's absolutely no confusion, the United States Department of Defense no longer looks to you for validation or approval. If you weren't aware, they've already begun phasing out your group. They've also set up more testing facilities in more countries than you could possibly imagine, none of which report to you. And they sure as hell aren't crying about a few broken dishes."

"Broken dishes? These are men, my men. And they aren't expendable just because you have a timeline. It doesn't work that way."

"But it does," Goodwin said. "If we don't get this

done within the next twelve months, someone else will. Do what you need to do, although for now, we are moving forward and will fix the issues as we go."

"I have to say—"

Interrupting yet again, Goodwin sat up straight. "This is going nowhere. Let's have someone with a bit of real data shed some light on these recent developments. You and I are too far removed from the actual day to day to see some of the more encouraging results."

Daniels nodded. He then turned to the young man seated to his right and spoke quietly into his ear. The young man stopped taking notes, stood, and moved out of the room.

"Okay," Daniels said. "What is it?"

"If I may... Ms. Briggs, our Senior Analyst, has done weekly projections based on our recent test subjects and the conclusions are extremely optimistic." Back to Daniels he continued. "I think she can inject some logic into what we've seen here today, and put your mind at ease regarding the direction we intend to follow over the next few years."

Sitting forward, Shannon glanced from Major Daniels over to Goodwin and then back to Daniels before standing and moving to the screen. Reaching for the remote, she scanned the footage and paused on the fourth video. "This is where we have an issue."

"Ms. Briggs?" Goodwin said. "Where is this

going?"

She stepped back and powered off the screen. Again turning from Goodwin to Daniels, she said, "Our problem is that it's mutating."

"What?" Daniels said.

"She's mistaken," Goodwin replied.

"No, the data is all there." Shannon stepped forward. "The newer test subjects are showing increased signs of neurologic detachment syndrome, but on an extremely amplified level."

Major Daniels smiled for the first time since they'd entered the room. "I understand the science behind what we intended to do; however, for this, I'm going to ask that you explain it to me like I'm a third grader.

Goodwin pushed away from his chair back and stood. "We're done here. I'll make sure you get a full report—"

"Marcus, this is the exact reason I made the trip down here today. The least you could do is allow me to hear what she has to say—she is *your* data analyst after all."

As Goodwin paused and breathed in through his nose, Shannon took the opportunity to continue. "Mr. Goodwin, Major Daniels has a valid argument." Her hands began to shake. "Three of the facilities have reported human to human transfer from the experimental group to the control group."

Through clenched teeth Goodwin spoke directly to her. "Yes, I am aware."

Turning her attention to Major Richard Daniels

she said, "This means we now have infected individuals who were never given the Ares injectable. It appears they were infected through the transfer of plasma."

Daniels cut his eyes at Goodwin. "Transmitted through blood?"

Shannon continued. "Yes. If early indicators are correct, the mutated cells responsible for shortening the synapse functions on the battlefield and in hand-to-hand combat have also decreased or completely removed certain inhibitors."

"This is why we're seeing men attacking, and in some cases, actually eating one another?"

"Yes." Shannon avoided eye contact with Goodwin and was surprised he hadn't yet stopped her. "As of the last two weeks, this glitch has resulted in the test subject's neurotic inability to feel or express impulse control. Those infected through blood to blood transfer essentially lose all ability to reason. They are controlled by only two impulses... feed and survive."

Waiting for her to finish, Goodwin moved the door, turned the handle, and held it open. Back to Major Daniels he said, "You've got what you came here for. If there's nothing else, I'm going to have to say goodbye. I'm already late for another meeting."

Major Daniels moved to Shannon, placed his hand on her shoulder and nodded. He then stepped around her to Goodwin, shook his hand, and stepped out of the room.

As Major Richard Daniels strode out into the

lobby, Marcus Goodwin slowly closed the door and returned to his seat. He motioned for Shannon to take a seat across from him and waited as she settled in. "So, that went a bit differently than I was expecting."

"Mr. Goodwin, I'm sorry. I did what I thought was the right—"

"Ms. Briggs, there is absolutely no reason to apologize. You know I'm actually glad Daniels has the full picture. As you were giving him the details, I realized something. First off, he probably has no idea what you told him, and second, he really has nowhere to go with that information. No one's going to listen to him anyway. He's a nobody on this project and at this point, more of a distraction than anything."

"But don't you think the others should know about what we're seeing?"

"Not all of it. And not just yet."

Shannon breathed out hard. "You're going to fire me, aren't you?"

"I'll admit, it did cross my mind. But the more you spoke, the more I realized where your special skills could be of use."

"Okay?"

"There is small assignment that I'm going to need you for. You will still be involved with the analytics from this project, just from a different location." Marcus Goodwin once again leaned back in his chair. "Tell me Ms. Briggs... how do you feel about small towns?"

Also by Jeff Olah

THE DEAD YEARS

A companion series build in the same world as the Best-Selling Post-Apocalyptic saga *The Last Outbreak.*
The End of the World was Only the Beginning.

Mason Thomas wasn't prepared when the devastation began that morning. No one was.

Six days ago reports of a mysterious illness began surfacing around the globe. The infection took hold quickly and destroyed everything in its path. The infected were seen attacking and actually devouring their victims. Those unfortunate enough to be caught out in the open were the first to fall.

Millions perished every hour.

The world was told not to panic, that there wasn't anything to worry about, that these were isolated events. This morning, as he fought to return to his family, Mason Thomas quickly realized that nothing was what it seemed... the world had been forever changed.

The Dead Years follows Mason Thomas, a separated husband and father of one, as he and a small group of survivors fight to stay alive at the end of the world.

THRESHOLD is their story.

(Turn the page for a sneak peek.)

Sneak peek of *The Dead Years*

THRESHOLD

1

No one knew how or where it all began. There were only rumors at first, spreading from one city to another. The infection took hold quickly. Many that became victims of the first wave were caught off guard by the unusual behavior of those infected. Millions perished with each day that passed and the number of survivors continued to dwindle as they desperately searched for places free of this hell.

The devastation was almost immediate. Law enforcement fell, utilities powered down and civilization was shattered within the first few weeks. With no structure left in the world, the few remaining sought to band together to fight and survive in this new existence.

They had no other choice...

Mason looked out over the floor in between sets and was somewhat caught off guard, and also a little amused as one of his favorite songs from high school started up through his headphones. He hadn't heard this for quite some time and figured his phone must be cycling through the deep reaches of his enormous playlist.

Just as the chorus set in, the music muted, signaling a call was coming through. Mason pulled the phone from his pocket to check who was calling. "April," he said aloud. He figured there must be something else she needed to harass him about and he wasn't going to ruin another workout just to satisfy her need to belittle him. He hit decline and lay back on the floor for another set of crunches.

Mason ran through his next set like a man on fire and lost all focus on the world around him. He often used his outside frustrations to fuel his high intensity workouts in the gym. This proved to be an effective tool in that he was able to push off his problems and at the same time get into top shape. The downside to all this was that his workouts, coupled with the time spent training clients, fueled the fire that resulted in his and April's separation three months ago.

Rolling forward and standing from his final set, Mason was surprised to see the weight room almost empty. He turned and noticed at least thirty people gathered outside the owner's office and as he got closer, he saw there was at least half that amount inside the office.

They seemed to be intently debating something as others hurried out the front exits of the gym and were headed for their cars. Mason asked one of the female on-lookers what was happening and just as she began to answer, his phone started to buzz, indicating he was getting a text message.

Again it was April.

Looking back at the woman standing directly in front of him, now appearing irritated, Mason said, "I apologize, what did you say?"

"The old folks home," she said.

"Yes..." Mason followed.

"They're killing each other... LOOK!"

Mason pushed his way through the diminishing crowd inside the office to get a glimpse of the television now directly in front of him.

The reporter standing in the hallway was in the middle of his report when he was overtaken by what appeared to be three individuals, all of whom were at least eighty years old.

Someone in the crowd said, "I am not sure what the hell they're taking, but I want some. Damn, I have never seen people that age move so fast."

The news station cut away just as the threesome overtook the reporter. The footage was disturbing in that it appeared as though they were not just attacking the reporter, but trying to devour him. The first crazed senior appeared to bite the reporter on the neck or face and just as they cut away it looked as though the others had the same intention.

The station went to a commercial and Tom the owner switched to another station covering a mysterious virus plaguing an emergency room with the same sort of crazy behavior; this time it wasn't senior citizens. The cameraperson appeared to be running from the hospital and dropped the camera just as he was trapped on all sides by the angry horde.

Mason looked over at Tom and watched as the remaining members either headed toward the doors or to the locker room, fearing the unknown. Tom stared at the screen a minute longer watching as the cameraman was torn to shreds by nothing more than the hands and mouths of the rabid individuals.

"Tom!"

"Yeah, what?" Tom said as though coming out of a fog.

"What the hell is happening?"

"How on earth would I know? It's on every damn station though... check it out."

As Tom flipped from one station to the next, every station—even the local cable channels—had coverage of these bizarre events taking place. Some of the network channels had started to go dark and this appeared to concern Tom.

"Mason, I'm closing up for the day. I need to get home; my wife is probably flipping out. I'm surprised she hasn't called yet. If you want to stay you can lock up, otherwise let's go."

"That's fine," Mason said. "I'm going to grab my bag and I'll just be a few minutes behind you."

Heading back toward the locker room, Mason turned and looked as Tom reached the front door.

"Tom, take care, I'll call you later."

Mason pulled the phone from his pocket and looked down remembering he had put April on ignore. "Great," he said.

Opening April's text, it read: *Check the news, I am really scared – PLEASE CALL ME!!!*

Mason sat in front of his locker and dialed April. Being the only remaining soul inside the gym felt a little creepy and not just because of the earlier images he had seen on the news. He always hated being here alone, especially when it was dead silent, and being here mid-afternoon with the place empty was just weird.

"Mason!" April answered on the forth ring.

"I'm just leaving the gym now," Mason said.

"Where are you headed?"

"Home... why?"

"Can you come here?" April asked. "I'm really scared and I need you."

"Where is Justin?" Mason asked.

"He's in school; I just checked out the window and everything is quiet."

Mason had never heard April this worried. He figured he would try to set her mind at ease. "I'm on my way to your place. Stay put and I'll be there in a few minutes."

"I will," April said, sounding a little less stressed. "Mason?"

"Yeah?"

"I just spoke to my Dad."

"Oh yeah, what did HE have to say about this?"

"He didn't say very much, although he made me promise him that we would get out of the city. TODAY!"

2

April hung up the phone and walked to the oversized bay window in her master bedroom. The home she had purchased eight years ago with Mason was supposed to be her dream home. Instead, it now reminded her of how hard she had been on him and how much she had let her father influence those bad times.

Thinking back to the better memories they shared, she remembered that they had decided on this home in particular because it overlooked not only the elementary, but also the middle and high schools. She persuaded Mason that if they stuck to the budget she outlined, they could literally watch their son grow from kindergarten to high school. She was sure her being overprotective did nothing to help their marriage. Mason would constantly let her know she needed to "loosen the reigns," especially since Justin was only a few months shy of his fourteenth birthday.

She desperately hoped Mason would arrive soon as she was freaked out after watching the news all day and talking to dear old dad.

"I guess we were spared," April said aloud as she looked out the window surveying both campuses, half trying to convince herself that she had nothing to worry about. No frantic people running around; in fact, the area seemed overly calm.

April made her way downstairs and into the kitchen just as the phone rang. She was sure it was Mason with some sort of an update, although upon checking the caller ID she noticed the call was coming from Justin's cell.

"Hello?" she quickly answered, trying to sounds as if she had not a care in the world.

"Mom, something weird is happening."

"What's going on?"

"All the teachers and staff were called to an emergency meeting and they haven't been back to the classrooms. It's been almost an hour now."

"Where are you?" April said.

"I walked out into the gym because the rest of the school is too loud. The other students are kind of just running around the halls. Mom, some of my friends are saying that there is a war that was started."

"Justin, I think they're just trying to scare you."

"Well, what IS going on? Why are all the teachers gone? Why haven't they come back?"

"I'm sure it's nothing. Just go back to cl..."

"Mom they're coming back, I gotta go."

April set the phone down and leaned back against the counter. She wanted Justin home and had to talk herself out of walking across the street to get him. She knew it would embarrass him and probably her as well.

April decided she would head back to the bedroom and sit at the window and watch, that way she could ease her mind and at the same time she would be ready to move if anything changed.

Even before she reached the window, April could see both parking lots start to fill with cars. Knowing there were no performances going on at the middle school today, she knew what was happening.

These parents were just as alarmed at the events of the day as she was; they were just less concerned with what the other parents thought of them.

"Screw it." Deciding she didn't care either, she dialed Mason again to let him know she was headed to the school to bring Justin home. She figured he could help her pack a few things and as soon as Mason arrived she would try to convince him that her father had some insight and they should heed his warning and head out of town.

Mason's phone went to voicemail once again. April typically would have just hung up, although she wanted him to know where she was if he got here before she got back.

"Mason, it's me, there is some weird stuff going on over at the school. I'm going over to bring Justin home. If you get here before I get back, the front door will be unlocked...Please hurry."

Before heading out, April grabbed the television remote and powered it up. She promised herself earlier that she would not watch any more coverage; however, she wanted to be sure there wasn't any new information.

Most of the network stations were now off the air. April flipped through the last of the local stations and came upon a disturbing feed that was playing on a loop showing a crowd of deranged people stampeding two middle aged women trying to get into the grocery store. She had to turn away and instantly hit the off button before she witnessed another second.

"What in the world is happening?"

3

April's father was a great man, sometimes too great for Mason to even stomach. He knew April loved him, but he also knew their marriage would continue to be an uphill battle as long as her father continued to add fuel to the fire.

Putting that aside, Mason knew better than to doubt this man. He knew April's father was some sort of military big shot; he just had no idea what kind. He figured it was better not to ask as it would have just led to some sort of discussion about why he couldn't measure up... it always did.

Mason dropped the phone into his backpack and headed for the exit. Walking down the row of treadmills, he made sure to turn down the lights in each section of the club. Rounding the corner and making his way out, Mason nearly tripped over the front desk chair as he couldn't believe the events taking place in the parking lot.

Through the giant glass windows that made up the front entrance of the club, Mason was horrified at what he was seeing. The club members and employees that had left only moments before were being run down and attacked by these savages that seemingly came out of nowhere. People were running, falling, and literally being torn apart by these things.

One of heavier men who only ten minutes before walked out the front door in a hurry to get to his car and vacate the area was now in a flat out sprint back toward the facility. He missed the step up onto the curb, went down hard, and slid face first into the glass entrance. The closed doors acted as a dead end for this man as three of those things were on him in seconds.

Mason's first reaction was to head toward the door and offer some sort of help, although the huge glass wall thirty feet in front of him was offering the only line of protection for him at this point. What kind of help was he going to offer anyway? These things seemed to be much stronger and looked as if they were literally feeding on anyone who came into their line of sight.

He figured there must be at least a hundred of them outside. While trying to come up with an escape plan, Mason knelt behind the desk not only to get out of sight, but also to block his view of the atrocious scene that lay before him. He had seen enough and needed to clear his head.

Mason needed to get to April and Justin; if her father was right, it had to be sooner rather than later. He looked back around the side of the desk and the focus of the mob had moved away from the parking lot and grown closer to the building. There had to be a dozen or so bodies pressed up against the glass while being torn apart.

He knew Tom kept a revolver in the locked cabinet under his desk. Mason got to his feet and made a break for the office. This time the crowd saw him and started pounding against the glass like a riot at a heavy metal concert. Mason slid into the office and behind the desk. "Not good!" He noticed the drawer open and the gun missing. Tom must have grabbed it on his way out. The pounding continued to escalate until there was a gigantic crash and Mason knew they were now inside.

Knowing his only option was to run; Mason grabbed his bag from the floor and noticed the revolver just outside the office. It must have fallen out of Tom's bag as he left in such a hurry.

Mason could hear the pounding footsteps getting closer as he grabbed the gun and continued to sprint toward the staircase at the back of the building that led to the roof. There was no other way out. Mason feared he would be trapped inside and eaten alive.

As he reached the stairs, the horde was only yards away from him and closing in fast. Mason refused to look back as he knew that would slow him down. As he pushed himself up the stairs with his legs he also used the handrail to pull himself toward the top in an attempt to move that much faster. Mason feared he would trip or miss a step and that would be it.

He didn't want to die here on this staircase. As he reached the top, he prayed the exit wasn't locked. He looked back and was pleased when he realized he had put some distance between himself and the deranged crowd. As he glanced over his shoulder before reaching the door, it looked as if those things were falling over each other to get up the stairs first.

Thankfully, the door to the roof was unlocked. As he burst through the door and onto the rooftop, Mason was momentarily blinded as the sun had broken through the clouds and was now drying what little rain had fallen.

As his sight became clear again, he twisted from side to side taking it all in. Every area, as far as the eye could see looked like a war zone. There were fires covering large parts of the city, car alarms sounding every few seconds, and screams of terror filling what little silence there was.

"What is this?" he said aloud.

Mason remembered the vacant furniture store to the right had closed six months ago and might still be untouched as he couldn't see any turmoil coming from that direction.

As the crowd reached the door to the roof, Mason put his head down and sprinted in the direction of the vacant store.

"*This may have been a terrible idea.*"

The distance he needed to jump now appeared much farther than he remembered. He knew if he didn't clear the large space between the two buildings that he would fall the thirty plus feet to the ground below and at the very least break his legs and become food for these monsters.

With only twenty feet before the edge and

adrenaline coursing through every ounce of his body, he could actually feel their footsteps coming from behind.

Mason dug in to increase his speed and with his last step he launched himself over the gap.

ABOUT THE AUTHOR

Jeff Olah is the author and creator of the best-selling series The Dead Years and The Last Outbreak. He writes for all those readers who love good post-apocalyptic, supernatural horror, and dystopian/science fiction.

His thirst for detailed story lines and shocking plot twists has been fueled over the years by stories from Cormac McCarthy, Ray Bradbury, and Stephen King. He also has a difficult time tearing himself away from character driven dramas like The Walking Dead and LOST.

He lives in Southern California with his wife, daughter, and five-year-old Chihuahua.

Connect with Jeff:
JeffOlah.com
Facebook.com/JeffOlah
JeffOlah.com/Newsletter

Made in the USA
Coppell, TX
28 July 2022